A WHITE CLOVER

Rivara Fall

A White Clover
Rivara Fall

A White Clover
Copyright © 2024 Rivara Fall

For more information, contact the author at rivarafall.com

The characters in this book are entirely fictional. Any resemblance to actual persons living or dead is entirely coincidental.

Printed in the United States of America

Paperback ISBN: 979-8-9899296-0-3
Hardcover ISBN: 979-8-9899296-1-0
Ebook ISBN: 979-8-9899296-2-7

Edited by: Jasmine Gower
Cover designed by: Rivara Fall
Author Website: rivarafall.com

Chapter 1
The Place of Omens

Her wings stood out in the dim grey atmosphere. Stone ruins sat among dead, twisted trees and broken statues of all sorts: man, monster, and those divine. Shadowed creatures wandered among the still air. Greyish stone beings with short, stubby wings; large, vacant eyes; thick, short limbs; and thin spaded tails. Each held their own unique charm. Some wide, some pencil-thin. Some had long, twisting tails reaching into the trees while others had none. Some wore scars, cracks in their stone façades. Broken and unapproached, left to wander their realm without a concern from either side.

A shadowed mass flew to the falling stone wall next to her. Its feet disturbed the surface, tumbling small rocks and dust to the ground. Curiosity, she assumed, unable to read any intent from its eyes. Stuck in shadows, unable to revert, its body strained to move, struggling not to fall and fade. She reached out a hand, gently touching the creature's face. Smooth stone began crawling over its form, solidifying it in its proper shape. The creature stretched its wings and tested its limbs, seemingly grateful of its repair.

"Rare to see white wings down here," a figure said, stepping out of the shadows. She stood tall, with soft light grey eyes that blended into the fog. Her hair was a deep, dark blood red that stood out against her dark clothing. A one-eyed gargoyle omen rested on her shoulder.

Airen remained calm. "They deserve no less treatment for what they are."

"A divine angel? Not so wary of things outside of your order?"

"Are you?"

Haven paused. Her expression softened as she reached out to a small omen. "I don't care for order, though I still get my enjoyment from messing with your kind."

Airen smiled. "What is your name?"

"Haven."

"Airen." She nodded at the omen on Haven's shoulder. "They seem to like you as well."

"Finicky and unpredictable at times, which is what I enjoy most about them. I call this one Scraps. He gets into his share of chaos but never strays too far."

The omen clambered onto the wall next to Airen, staring at her with a single hollowed eye. The other had been replaced by deep cracks.

"What happened to his face?" Airen asked.

"I don't know. He's always been like that. I tried to fix him a few times, but they won't budge."

"May I try?"

"If he'll let you."

2

Airen reached out toward the omen, slowly placing her fingers against his face. His smooth stone surface let out no heat or cold, just as the air around it. Energy radiated through her fingertips, though his stone did not react. The cracks remained. "Strange..."

Haven stepped closer. "I have an eye for odd things."

"You refer to Scraps as he?"

"It feels correct, not really sure why."

"Surrounded in mystery."

"At least my existence is interesting."

"Very."

Almost cat-like, Airen thought, smiling as the creature rubbed against her hand. *Same size even... Why do you follow her?* "I believe I've seen him before."

"I will admit to a bit of lurking. A few angels visit every now and then just to see what it's like down here. Few frequently visit."

"You were watching me?"

"No more than the omens."

"Well, I am admittedly glad for the company."

"I'm done with my tasks for the day and wanted some peace and quiet."

"Do other demons spend time here?"

"A couple. They usually come to visit a statue or old place, something fallen. Some seek out the things that inspire them. Others come to visit old friends."

"Like a graveyard."

3

"I guess they do have similarities. Both are quiet and still. A place where both of our kinds can belong."

Belong... Is that why you linger here? Airen stepped closer. "Can I ask what you think of me? I haven't had the chance to meet a demon before."

Haven smiled and raised an eyebrow. "You're curious and don't seem too afraid. I would be more cautious with others that you meet. I'm not as violent as most."

"Why not?"

"There has to be a reason. I'm not just going to go around blindly thrashing at things. Even evil must have some sort of order to it."

"Curious... Have you met Michael? He tends to think every demon would harm us at any opportunity. I'm curious how he would react to you."

"If he is as one-sided as you say, then he probably wouldn't give me a chance to speak before attacking me."

"Well, that is a fair thought."

"Do you believe him?"

"No, I prefer to see things for myself."

"How far are you willing to go to see?"

"As far as I need."

"Some might take that as a challenge, see how long it takes to make you fall. Drown you in your curiosity."

"Then I guess I'd have to take it as a challenge as well, see how long I can hold out against you."

"I'm not here for your wings. I'm here to relax."

"Do I keep you from that?"

"No. You don't seem the type to get into fights. How long have you been an angel?"

"A year. Most of my time was spent in the Halo. Izeah was quick to see my divinity."

"Stuck reading and honing your abilities?"

"Yes."

"It's better to get out right away and get a feel for the reality in front of you."

"I assume you weren't bound to books when you were cast?"

"No..."

She doesn't seem bothered or concerned to be standing three feet from an opposing being. I wonder why she has her wings hidden. Perhaps a question for later. "Well, it seems I was in good fortune tonight. Will I see you here again?"

"Probably, if you are so keen to keep hanging around."

"I like talking with you."

"I feel the same." Scraps darted down the path, fluttering his wings with helpless clumsiness. "Looks like I have somewhere to be. I'll see you around, divine."

Chapter 2
The Shuck of Luck

The streets were poorly paved, flooded with uneven puddles and muddy cracks. The lights were flickering from bent posts, straining to allow those of normal eyes to see. Though the city was vast and bright during the day, its nights were suffocating and dark. No stars could be seen. The moon hid behind the skyscrapers' ever-looming shadows.

Airen stood in the rain, watching a small group rush into a building, shifting their eyes to the surrounding shadows. *So much fear at this hour.*

"It's following me. The damn Shuck is following me!" a man yelled from a nearby window. His eyes shifted around the room as he paced with uneven footsteps.

A woman peeked out of the plain tan curtains, scanning the empty streets. "It's just a dog, Ed."

"No...it's some sort of freak! I can't deal with this. Why won't it go away?"

"Dogs don't just wander around. They pick a territory to defend."

"It's not a dog!"

"What else would it be? You're just tired. Go to sleep."

"No, it's going to come for me...eat me or something..."

"Ed..."

"No!"

Airen turned back toward the dark alley. "Why do they fear you so strongly?"

A solid black figure stepped out into the flickering light. Long, pointed ears curved out of its dog-like head. Its body was thick and smooth, lacking a tail. Its legs bent down, flattening out into human hands and feet. It left no sound or footprints in its path.

She reached down, gently resting her hand on its head. "You are not harming them."

The omen sat next to her, leaning into her touch. Its eyes focused on the window. Its ears turned to face the maddened cries.

"You don't believe me. Why don't you believe me!?" The man's fear was turning to rage, his arms swung around the room. The woman jumped back, letting out a cry of fear.

Airen summoned her divine staff. It glowed blue and white with three sections along the handle. Both ends curled outward, reaching back together to hold a rhombus shape. She lifted it toward the window, listening to the woman's silent prayer. *Please, make it stop. I'm afraid.*

The man's eyes blurred. His rage subsided as he fumbled onto the couch. The woman let out a sigh of relief. *Thank you.*

"Dream away your fears," Airen said. "Sometimes they bring luck." She returned her hand to the omen's head. "Where to now?"

The creature turned down the street, leading her further into the dark. A car drove by, unaware of their presence. The waters splashed though didn't drench their figures. She wondered if the omen knew the touch of the rain or the sun on its surface, if they could feel—if only they could say.

A man stared down at his phone with a look of uncertainty. His footsteps were rushed and uneven. His thoughts were far from his body, unconcerned of the rain or darkness. Unaware of the approaching pair of lights. The shuck stepped forward, revealing his form. The man glanced up for a moment, then jumped back and dropped his phone, staring at the creature in a panic. The car raced by, causing him to lose his footing. Cold, muddy water soaked his shoes and pants, sending a chill though his body. He stared down at the pavement beneath his feet, finally acknowledging his surroundings. *What... Did I just...* His eyes shot upward, though the beast had vanished.

Airen had grown accustomed to being unseen, those familiar eyes of uncertainty all mortals showed when given a single glance of those beyond. No matter if they showed fear, awe, or curiosity, they would always have the same wide-eyed stare as they tried to reason with their senses.

The shuck turned its large ears and stared down the road. "What do you hear?" Airen asked. "Another?"

Thirty minutes they walked, calm and quiet. Cold winds battered the edge of the park, unable to reach them through the thick trees. She could remember the feeling, the sting of cold air and the ache of chilled droplets against her skin, things that no longer plagued her. The clouds closed and let out a fierce rumble. Faint cries fought the storm for her attention. Somewhere in the dark shade of the park, beneath a tall tree, was a small figure shivering in muddied cloths.

"Poor boy." Airen revealed her form and stepped closer to the child. "Are you lost?"

The boy looked up and wiped his eyes. "Y...yes."

"Would you like me to help you get home?"

"It's too dark."

"Don't worry." She gestured toward the shuck. "My friend here can see just fine."

The boy reached out to pet the shadowed creature. "What's his name?"

Well, they don't really have names... Perhaps I'll call them... "Luck."

The boy smiled and stood up. "My name is Dustin."

"Airen." She reached out to take his hand.

"Mom won't let me get a dog. She says they cause too much trouble."

"They can be mischievous."

"Does Luck get into trouble?"

"Sometimes, though most of the time it is just a misunderstanding."

"I don't mean to get into trouble either... Mom says I get too distracted."

"You are still growing and figuring out the world. You're bound to scatter your attention across all the interesting new things."

"Like pigs! The new neighbor has a pig that they walk around like a dog."

"That is interesting."

"Dustin? Dustin!" A woman yelled.

"Mom!" The boy ran across the road, leaping into his mother's arms.

"Where were you? Are you ok?"

"I got lost in the dark. The nice lady and her dog helped me..." He turned back toward the park. Both figures had disappeared.

"What lady?"

"They...walked me home. I told them about the pig."

The woman stared into the trees. Not a single movement or sound. No trace of life. "Well, seems they left. Come on, let's get you inside."

Airen stood across the street, watching them return to the warmth of their home, listening to the boy's excited tale.

"Dogs can see in the dark, Mom. If I had my own, I'd never get lost."

"Unless it decides to run off too, Dustin."

"They know their way home. It could keep me safe."

"Just eat your food and get to bed. No more running off after dark."

Airen closed her eyes.

"*No more running off after dark. Strange things wander the park at night.*"

"*Ok, Papa.*"

The scent of candles and soup. The feel of a soft rug beneath her feet and a fluffy small dog at her side. *Will I always remember? Decades, centuries from now? I hope I will. I would like to.*

Something smooth brushed against her hand, returning her attention to the dark evening air. "I was thinking...reminiscing. I was also one to wander as a child, though not nearly as far."

The rain slowly faded, exposing the dark sky above. Though the stars were hidden for mortal eyes, shielded by the city lights, she could see each one with perfect clarity. Bright and fierce colors that flickered and shifted like calm waves rolling across the galaxy.

"Do you see them as well?"

The omen looked up, staring at the vast sky above them. The colorful stars reflected in its eyes, dancing around its view. It nodded in agreement.

"I'm glad. It's a beautiful sight. A shame people don't get to enjoy it with us." She sat next to the creature, continuing to enjoy the colors shining above. "Thank you for accompanying me. Tonight, you are luck."

Chapter 3
A Cage of Forty Years

The man rested on his knees, praying through the bars of his cell. The night air brought cold chills through the tiny window. Airen stood nearby, hiding herself. She focused on his words. Praise of the almighty, forgiveness and hope. His words strained with exhaustion and fear. A dreary look came upon his face as he shuffled into his bunk.

A familiar voice echoed through the hallway. Airen turned and slowly made her way toward the sound. Most others had already slipped into slumber. Their misfortunes continuing through their nightmares. Even in sleep, the place could not be escaped.

Haven sat in a cell, on a bunk, with a confident smile on her face and a lighter in her hand. An older man sat across from her, rubbing his brow. "Evening, Haven," he said in a familiar tone.

"Joe."

"Once again a reminder to my wrongs?"

"Six people, Joe. It's worth a few words."

He sighed. "It is."

"Still given up? Not even going to argue?" She flicked on the lighter, messing with the flame.

"I'm too tired. Been in here for...forty years with you stopping by once a week to chat. They all think I'm crazy."

"You stopped caring thirty years ago."

"You didn't. You're still showing up."

"I don't have that many jobs."

"Almost done with this one? I'm not going to live forever."

"We could certainly try. I'm not done tormenting you yet."

He chuckled. "I've got to stop putting ideas in your head, or I'll never see the end of this."

Scraps lingered in the corner of the cell. Joe's eyes followed the shadow, unrest mixed with familiarity. Nightmares, ghosts, evil spirits—few mortals called them omens. Joe had been acquainted with this particular shape for the last forty years. First in his dreams, then in the unescapable grasp of reality as it accompanied Haven to her visits. Though still haunting, bringing a sense of unease wherever it lingered, Joe had learned to accept it. The creature that disturbed his rest, serving as a constant reminder. Though he saw only one, six shadows lingered in his head.

"Do you understand them yet?" Haven asked.

"Don't reckon I do. If I did, something would change, right?"

"You'll figure it out." She stood up and tossed the lighter into his lap. *Not long old man...* She wasn't sure how she knew. Few others could feel the impending shadow of

13

demise slowly creeping up on unsuspecting mortals. The feeling lingered in the air, barely reaching her senses, never knowing what or when, just soon. *Hopefully not as harsh as the ones you caused.* She walked out of the cell, fading from sight. Bright blue eyes caught her attention. "Tending to sinners now?"

"A miracle was due," Airen said, stepping closer.

"Which one?"

"Toby Red."

"The new guy? Must still be clinging to grace."

"He was incarcerated after an accident. Tomorrow he will be freed based on new evidence."

"Don't let the word get out," she joked. "Not everyone can pray themselves out of prison." She opened a portal to the Omen Lands.

Airen followed her through the cold, lifeless air. "Can I ask what happened to Joe?"

Haven leaned back against a crumbling stone wall. "He was your typical wild, drugged-up kid. One day a guy sold him and his buddies bad drugs. He went into a mad rage, didn't know what he was doing. Ended up killing his friends and three curious neighbor kids."

"Hard to redeem the death of six, even as an accident."

"People hit bad choices every day. Some die, some live in regret or confusion. Bliss to those that don't understand enough to worry about it."

"I have yet to meet a human without fear."

"Go visit the north wilderness some time. They'll fight the freezing winds for fun."

"You know them far more deeply than the other after-beings I've met."

"I've had time. Humans can be better company than demons. They aren't made for something specific, performing the same trivial tasks that we do. Demons will go for one of three options depending on how much blood they want to get on their hands. Humans will reach for a hundred."

"Their freedom does create intrigue."

"Odd to think, gaining such power also narrowed our paths."

"You don't seem the type to only go for three options."

"No, I'd rather have more to my existence."

"So would I."

Haven smiled. "Care for an adventure then? Why don't I go ahead and show you some of the more defiant humans."

"The northern lands you were speaking of?"

Haven opened a portal of grey swirling smoke and offered her hand. "If you dare to trust a demon."

Airen smiled and took her hand, closing her eyes. The portal shifted. The grey stone walls were replaced by dark green trees covered in a blanket of snow.

"You won't have to hide your wings out here," Haven said. "Humans are known to dismiss slight oddities if they have strong enough focus on their own reality. The slight silhouette of your feathers won't be noticed by their eyes. All they'll see are the thick flakes of snow."

"I imagine yours would stand out drastically. I have yet to see them."

"Well, can't open them now..." Haven led her to a small clearing in the trees, sheltered from the nearby winds. "These people know exactly where to stand, what to wear, and when to move," she said, watching people huddled around a small fire, laughing and drinking.

Airen stepped closer. "They act as though the surrounding forest isn't trying to kill them."

"The people up here have to grow up in natural hardships. They must survive through childhood. They learn the harsh realities of the world and how to push through it, leaning heavily on prideful family traditions and fuck you energy."

"They truly aren't afraid."

"They aren't raised to be."

"I haven't dealt with many from this area before."

"They grow up with more confidence. Less need to pray for guidance, though many still do."

"I wonder how they would be if we weren't here, if there weren't outside things influencing their lives."

"I'm sure they would still be here, laughing and drinking around the fire, telling stories and letting out frustrations. The humans that don't believe in us aren't all that different than those that do."

"Fair. It is nice to know that they can be happy without us."

"We haven't always been around to help and hinder them."

"I know."

A man stumbled into the fire. Airen stepped forward. Haven grabbed her arm. The group laughed and helped him up, throwing his flaming coat into the snow. Their eyes were calm and content, not a hint of fear.

"See," Haven started, "they do fine on their own if they're taught to survive without paranoia. They see the fire, know what it's going to do, don't stress about it, and take care of the situation."

"If more people were like that, I wouldn't have much to do."

"Technology is changing our tasks. Perhaps one day it will guide humans better than we ever could."

"Then they wouldn't need us."

"No."

Airen smiled. "I can picture little flying robots following people around, doing angelic tasks. Perhaps some are sabotaged to do evil acts instead."

"People create their own angels and demons."

"Sounds a bit creepy, especially if they talked to them. A little robot hovering over your shoulder, whispering guidance to you."

"Would give a new meaning to the whole 'angel and demon on your shoulder' thing," Haven said.

17

"I wonder what the Lord would think of that."

"Would use less magic. The Lord's plan was about giving energy back to the mortals."

"Now they are starting to manipulate it in their own way. Definitely less taxing to use their science than our magic."

"Their science is limited, for now at least."

"For now..." Airen laughed.

"What?"

"What if there was a divine intervention hot line?"

"666 for demons, 777 for angels. Fuck, that's funny. Hmm, who should I call for advice today: Mom, a therapist, or an after-being?"

"Michael would have a heart attack."

"I know some demons that would love it."

"I don't know, I think I'd prefer not to have a phone," Airen said. "Would they even work in all of the realms?"

"No, the magic interferes with them."

"Perhaps people will one day make something that can work alongside our magic."

Haven turned back toward the group, watching them pull out instruments. "Perhaps, but for now most of them are just along for the ride."

The forest slowly filled with music as the sun dimmed. Their laughter turned to song. Their stumbling footsteps turned to dance. The fire roared between them, unifying them to one spot. A single anchor of safety.

"What are they singing about?" Airen asked.

"Roughly translates to 'fuck mother nature, we follow the call of our adventurous hearts.'"

Airen laughed. "I think we all need that kind of energy every once in a while."

"Your version is hanging out with me."

"It would seem."

"How about we have a little fun of our own then?" She drew a circle in the snow with her foot then reached out a hand. "Come here."

Airen took it. "Why?"

Haven pulled her to stand across the circle. "The point of their dance is to show off, tease the fire in a way, and try not to get burned."

Airen watched the people dancing closer and closer to the flames, moving just fast enough to avoid its touch. Haven moved to the left, keeping hold of her hands. Airen tried to focus and move in a similar pattern. *She's pretty good at this. Me...not so much... She does have a pretty smile and very unique eyes.*

The snow gently crunched beneath their feet. The song sped up. More people gathered around the fire, singing along, jumping, and yelling with excitement. Airen's feet fumbled, sending her colliding onto Haven.

"And we're toasted," Haven said, smiling. "Don't want to fall if you ever go dancing with the mortals. Would be a little alarming when you don't catch fire."

"Is that a personal experience of yours?"

"No, it happened to a friend of mine... I might have pushed him."

Oh, I'm still on top of her. She has an arm around me. I guess she doesn't mind.

One of the men called out. Haven turned back toward the group. "Shit, they saw us. Time to disappear."

Airen stood. "Don't want to chat with them?"

"Don't really want a bottle thrown at me again. That might have been the same group that watched my friend fall into the fire. We ended up getting chased through the woods with angry people throwing things at us, calling us demons."

"Well, they were accurate at least."

"Very."

Clouded grey smoke covered their figures until they sat in the familiar silence of the Omen Lands. Airen looked around. "Why here?"

"I prefer it. I get enough of rowdy demons dealing with my usual jobs."

"Fair enough. Have any more to do today?"

"No, but I do have to help a friend."

"Then perhaps I'll see you again later."

"Perhaps you will."

Chapter 4
The Gates of the Halo

The golden gate stood tall, beaming out among the clouds. Four large pillars stood between two thick slabs of clear crystal. If the sun was just right, it would glow a rainbow of colors bringing unending brightness to the surrounding area. There were those who spent most of their time at the gates, waiting for the lights to bring in new arrivals. Angels would gather to converse, telling stories of their own beginnings to those anew.

Many wore the soft robes and simple shoes, though still with their own unique charm. Colors swayed above the clouds, standing out against their wearer's stark white feathers. For him, a simple orange shirt, white sweatpants, and a kind, warm smile would suffice. His large white wings remained folded behind him, gently brushing against the clouds surface. Izeah was one to frequent the gates, wandering among the small crowds, listening to tales, and giving guidance when needed. None knew exactly when a new angel would be cast, though many would still spend their days waiting, so that none would feel lost or alone.

An older woman laughed and gestured for Izeah to join them. "Here is the one who first spoke to me. I had no idea I was speaking to an archangel."

"I have no need for status," Izeah said. "I would rather everyone see me as an equal."

"You are too kind, Izeah, a true divine! We should all aspire to show your kindness."

"Your aspirations are your own. Follow whatever path brings you true happiness."

A larger man laughed. "To wake and immediately be met with smiles and laughter, that is what I wish for all our brethren. We shall be the best welcoming committee yet!"

Izeah smiled and continued to wander. He knew every face, every name, even who they were before they died. He made a point to introduce himself to all arrivals at some point, asking about their lives and ambitions. The more interesting stories he would later recall to his brother.

No matter how many times he looked upon its tall golden structure, it would always bring a grin to his face. He was one of few that had not been cast by gate, one who had never laid upon its glass, though he would always bring a smile to those that had, the winged figures that now looked to him for guidance.

His eyes shifted toward a lone figure by the border. "Airen?"

"Hello, Izeah."

"Lingering in the background again?" He followed her gaze toward a group of clouded figures. They were often mistaken for shadows or strange cloud formations due to odd winds, though mortals rarely saw them. Most gathered around places of angels and demons, pacing and scratching at the border, unable to enter. Their bodies merged with the surrounding clouds, reaching with ever shifting arms and staring through empty holes in their skulls. Some paced aimlessly, while others stared in stillness, reaching for an unknown destination.

"Why do they want in?" Airen asked, turning back toward Izeah.

"They are said to be caused by broken miracles, those that were cast too late, or were not as divine as intended. Some speculate that they wish to return to those that cast them. We have been trying to research them. They have been growing in numbers lately."

"Should we be concerned?"

"They do not seem to cause harm, nor can they enter the Halo. It is more a point of curiosity."

"They look...oddly human, like ghostly skeletons."

"Perhaps they reflect those that they were supposed to belong to." Izeah turned away. "If they do become a threat, I'm sure the bullish beasts will contain them well enough."

"Do we have any ideas how to remove them?"

"We've tried a few things, but they don't respond to our magic. We are considering trying some human customs for getting rid of ghosts or evil spirits."

23

"Could I explore today? I would like to see some of these customs."

"Of course. If anything catches your eye, please let me know."

Airen closed her wings, fading them from sight as she stepped through a portal. *I know just the place to start. Should be right around the corner.*

The streets were lively with early morning business. People rushed toward their morning destinations without a care or concern for the white-haired woman wandering into the apothecary shop.

A tall, energetic man stood behind the counter with a beaming smile. He wore a bright orange and pink robe. His skin was covered in brightly colored tribal tattoos and symbols for luck. "Ah, Airen, good to see you again." He walked around the counter, giving her a hug.

"You remember me."

"I have impeccable memory. Now, what brings you here today?"

"I'm curious to learn more about spirits. They weren't a big part of my culture growing up. I know people have different versions of their beliefs."

"Each community has their own ideas, methods of communication, rituals, or customs that they practice, all revolving around the idea of spirits. I was raised in a small village in Africa. Our beliefs were based on our ancestors. Spirits were usually seen as souls that were trying to help guide us through life, though most people around here are a bit more ominous about the whole thing, so many come here to find ways to rid themselves of their spirits."

"What methods usually work?"

"Incense is a popular choice. The more religious folk will ask the local priests to bless the place. Some people use special communication boards or cards to try and talk to them."

"Anything you recommend?"

"I prefer to just let them be. They don't bother me." He turned toward an older couple at the door. "Would you excuse me for a moment? I have to fetch their delivery from the back."

"Of course."

Colors were beyond abundant as each section was painted to represent a different part of the world. The shelves were decorated with crystals, animal skulls, statues, books, tiny bottles of various liquids, cards, plants, and powders. Everything was in place, perfectly labeled, often with small descriptions for use underneath. Airen wandered around the room, reading about whatever items caught her eye.

"Morning, divine. It is weird seeing you with your wings hidden."

"Haven." Airen turned toward her and smiled. "I have yet to see yours."

"I don't need them out right now."

"Here for a task?"

"No, I like to hang around and listen. People come in here with all sorts of stories."

"You know Dejen?"

"Pretty well. We joke around about me being a demon. He doesn't actually believe it, but it's good fun."

"He is quite an interesting soul. Calm and reasonable without a shred of anger or fear."

"He grew up traveling. Decided to embrace difference." She picked up a small jade dragon statue. "He respects all cultures and beliefs. One of the better mortals."

"Do you think he will one day become like us?"

"He would be far more fitting as an angel. Hell, I'd even pin him as a potential divine."

"Then you can surprise him with your wings, that you were, in fact, not lying about being a demon."

"I'd like to see the look on his face."

"Ah, Haven," Dejen said, walking up to the pair, "also here about spirits?"

"Was here for entertainment but decided to pester this angel instead."

Dejen let out a chuckle. "Ah, Haven, I was beginning to worry you didn't have any friends aside from me."

She nudged Airen's shoulder. "I have more than she does."

"She's new to the area. I'm sure she'll outmatch you soon enough. She is lovely as ever." He gave Airen a wink.

"Can't deny that."

He raised an eyebrow, studying Haven's expression. *Interesting...* "Do you have any more questions, Airen?"

"Not at the moment."

"You are always welcome to stop by any time. In fact, come by for dinner soon, I'd love to hear how you two met. I'm sure it's an interesting tale."

"Sounds nice."

Haven put an arm around Airen. "Dinner with a demon and angel—quite the story for you, Dejen."

"Perfect for business too, ha ha."

"It does sound nice," Airen added.

Haven let go of her. "Away from the prying eyes of your judgmental family."

"You're more fun."

"Glad I get to satisfy your curiosities."

Dejen grinned. "A perfect couple." He turned toward a group that had just walked in. "Ah, I'll leave you to it."

"Did he call us... Does he think we're together?" Airen asked.

"I guess he assumed I was flirting when I called you an angel. It's not too out of the ordinary."

"You often flirt with women?"

"Occasionally, though you're the only one I call divine."

"One to toy with mortal hearts?"

"No, just casual conversation. I don't get too close." She opened the door, following Airen out. The morning air was bright, still warming up. The clouds were sparse, brightly

27

contrasting the sharp blue haze of the sky. "You were researching spirits?"

"Not quite. Do you know much about the illfell? They have been growing in numbers around the gates."

"Just by the gates?"

"A few wander the border. One has become quite large. We've been having issues containing them."

"Send omens after them," Haven said. "They attack illfell."

"Really?"

"Cercaius wanted my help trying to get some weird-looking ones away from the fourth gate a while back. Scraps had just started following me around. He went right for them. Now we keep omens by the gates. Haven't had any illfell problems since."

"Interesting. It does make sense. There were no illfell when the old gods had reign."

"They most likely eradicated them before they could cause problems."

"I pray to them any time I need guidance or feel uncertain."

"I didn't know angels still did that."

"Not many," Airen said. "Most will seek the guidance of an archangel or word of the Lord."

"I'm not one for prayer."

"Have you ever spoken to the Lord?"

"I don't think so, but I have spoken to the old gods."

"I like to keep them company, even though they are still and silent. They still influence the world by listening to prayers and guiding omens."

"I wonder what they would think seeing us together without conflict."

"I'm sure they would be entertained."

"Have you told your friends about me?" Haven asked.

"It hasn't come up yet."

"A little daring, I see."

"Izeah wants me to gather my own opinions on the world. He isn't one to push or pry."

"Still a little dangerous, hanging around a demon without backup. Not scared that I'll harm you?"

"No, I'm not," Airen said with a smile.

"Think you could take me in a fight?"

"Probably not. I should get back home, tell Izeah about your illfell advice."

Haven watched her disappear through a cloud of smoke. *You probably could, to be honest...*

Chapter 5
Black Books

Airen's hand gently ran across the wall. *Metal and stone, always cold and damp when the light never touches it, yet nothing compares to its heat searing to the touch when the sun beams down upon it. I wonder how long it's been since these have seen the sun.*

The sound of scurrying stone claws and wings echoed down the hall, getting closer. A small gargoyle figure morphed out of the shadow of an open door. Airen turned to face them. "Scraps? Visiting anyone in particular?"

He jumped up into the air, leading her down the hall toward the only lit cell. Joe sat on the bed, reading a small black book.

"I told you that thing isn't accurate," Haven said, appearing in the shadows.

"I know, but it's still important to me. It's what I was raised with. Helped guide me."

"Through false words and assumptions."

"It does help to keep some of us calm... If it's so inaccurate, why allow it to stay?"

"An agreement. It benefits both sides in different ways, so we all agreed to let the books continue influencing mortals."

"I guess I can understand that. There are many that use it to harm and judge others." He set it on the bed. "Are you going to ask?"

"Do I need to?"

He sighed. "No, I don't... Sometimes I wonder if I ever will."

"Do you still see them?"

He closed his eyes. "In every dark moment. I honestly thought they were haunting me until you showed yourself."

"It's easy to madden mortals by being vague in our torment and let you come up with your own twisted ideas of what's going on."

"Do you talk to other mortals?"

"Not typically. Thought I'd try something new with you."

"Why? Why me?"

Her mind slipped into feelings of familiarity, the comfort of an old friend. *I don't know...* "You were smart enough not to completely freak out when you saw me. There wasn't any reason not to, honestly. Either you would have gone completely mad, or I'd just get to be more direct about your torment. Seems to be working out pretty well."

"Going to talk me to madness? Does seem pretty maniacal."

"Half the time you mortals drive yourselves mad on your own. I just need to find the tipping point."

"What's mine?"

"You already know."

"I...thought it was the shadows, that little creature that hides in the corner of my eye... But now I think that's only a piece. It's the shadows that aren't there, the ones I don't understand. I feel like they should be tormenting me, helping to drive my execution. Being kept alive here knowing full well my wrongs and having no way to apologize to them...that seems tormenting enough." He reached for the bible. "It is weird—people praise angels and their ideals as things bright and pure, yet so many of our godly bibles are made with dark covers."

"There's dark in everything, Joe, even angels."

"Do any of them visit here?"

Haven turned toward the figure hiding in the hallway. "More often than you'd think."

"Just never for me."

"Do something holy, and maybe they'll think about it." She stood up. "Later, Joe."

"Night, Haven." He reached for the light.

"Whose watching who now?" Haven asked, stepping into the hallway and fading from mortal sight.

"I'm glad we're allowed to interact with them," Airen responded. "It would be far less interesting if we weren't. I know there was discussion about limiting our contact with mortals."

"Yeah, I heard about that meeting. Demons don't follow orders enough for it to be worth it. It would just cause a disadvantage to your kind."

"Can I ask you something?"

"Yes?"

Airen looked back at Joe. "Have you ever cursed him?"

"I don't need to. Simply existing drives him mad enough. Hell, tell any religious mortal their bible isn't accurate, and they lose it. No curse required."

"A mortal wrote it, correct?"

"Yes, one who had spoken with a fallen."

"That explains the...rough translations."

"The cross on the front was originally meant to represent a combination of our staffs. Angel and demon."

"Makes sense, since it benefits both sides."

"Yeah, though mortals didn't take it that way. They still had to come up with a book that counters it. They assume they know everything. Everything has to have a side or angle, even us."

"It isn't as strict as they think. We just want them to thrive and be happy. At least my kind do. We don't care about the specifics as long as they get along."

"Do they still require you to read the bible when you're cast?"

"Yes," Airen responded. "I was told demons have to as well."

"Yeah, though most of them are argumentative about it. They'd rather burn people or plot to overthrow a peaceful leader than get stuck researching human beliefs."

"I've seen angels bemoan it too. Those that are more eager to get out and start making a difference."

"Impatient and energetic. We all have those. They cause most of our fighting, assuming enemies and battling head-to-head for their cause. They'll get the whole balance thing eventually. Have anything else to do here?"

"No, I'm done."

"Where are you headed next?" Haven asked.

"Izeah wanted me to read something, but he isn't very particular about timing."

"Want to waste a couple hours with me?"

"Doing what?"

Haven opened a portal leading to a sandy shore. "I assume you have more questions, unless you've found another demon to hang around with."

Airen sat down in the shade. "I haven't. I've seen a couple in the Mortal Realm, usually following a human around, causing heinousness."

"Didn't have the urge to walk up to any of them?"

"They were busy, and I am smart enough to observe before walking up to a stranger."

"Fair enough."

"And you, do you often walk up to angels?"

"Just the interesting ones."

Airen raised an eyebrow. "You speak to others as well?"

"I've run into a couple on occasion. You are the only one I have actual conversations with, except the fallen."

"I guess you would run into more of them in the Omen Lands."

"Some are interesting company. Others are just lost."

"Gabriel likes to talk about the equality of our work. There are always the same number of angels that there are demons, even among the fallen."

"Yes, honestly some of the fallen seem to be wiser than the archangels and archdemons. They live in the divide, understand more views. Granted, they are still bound to the same base rules."

"I assume yours are similar to ours."

"They are. Tasks are primary, though you can harm mortals that you run into if needed. Don't touch mortals with your staff. No moving mortals through portals or bringing them to other realms. That one was learned the hard way."

"Oh?" Airen asked.

"A demon tried to bring a mortal home. The man was...deformed...by the magic."

"Deformed?"

"Trust me, you don't want the details."

"Does it happen with portals too?"

"Not to the same extent. We used to be allowed to move mortals back when their population was much lower and they were more fragile. Moving them helped save populations or torment those that deserved it. Being able to portal a human into a prison would be helpful for you, but people these days wouldn't be able to handle that mentally with the lack of magic in their lives."

"It would make things easier, but I understand the confusion having some random person appear in a jail cell."

"Prisons don't work anyways, not for their betterment." Haven closed her eyes, feeling the warm breeze flow through her hair. "How many of them would give anything to do what we can. Magically appear in a place like this, especially those like Joe, trapped in a cage for so long."

"If only he hadn't killed those people. He honestly seems like a good man."

"He is, he just never got a chance to prove it."

Chapter 6
Scraps of Luck

At times, angels would influence those below, guiding them toward grand structures of their own, filled with life and vibrance. Their places of peace, a small reflection of the Halo. Airen found herself staring at such a building. A grand library at the center of a city. Smooth stone and marble glad to show its strength. Hand-carved doors and windows fixed with stained glass images of battles, animals, the stars, and the gods that once reigned. *Quite like the library in the Halo. Galea must have had some influence on the architect that designed it... Oh, what do we have here?*

A muffled yell burst out of the main door. Haven walked out. "You really like this place, huh?" she asked the small omen following her.

Airen smiled. "Causing trouble, you two?"

Haven gestured toward Scraps. "He really likes looking at the books."

"Really?" Airen reached out to pet the omen. "He's the troublesome one, then?"

"Sometimes."

"I did have an uncle that thought gargoyles watched people."

"Well...technically he was right."

"He would be very happy to hear that. Want to walk with me?"

"Anywhere in particular?"

"Wherever we end up." Airen looked around the street, watching people walk by. "Their eyes shift with emotions, caught in their tasks and conversations. Even those that dart around with paranoia have no concern for us. No idea that shadows linger around us. Shadows both far darker and lighter than the ones behind their eyes. What do you think they would say if the mortals knew we were here?"

"Something religious, confused ramblings perhaps."

"We do allow their odd beliefs."

"Helps keep them creative. What they don't know drives them into a frenzy of curiosity. They try more, test more boundaries over things they know little about."

A large dog-like shadow shifted in the alley. Airen turned and nodded toward the creature. "Hello, Luck."

"Know this one in particular?" Haven asked.

"We spent a night wandering the city, answering prayers."

"You sure are good at telling these guys apart."

"I have a gift for details."

"Won't be easy to hide things from you, then."

"This one wants us to follow them."

"Do you often chase omens?"

"They lead to curious places."

"Fair enough." The shuck darted toward a flaming building. Haven stopped in front of it. "Well, not something you see every day."

"A fire department on fire... How?"

"Humans are always doing weird shit. How often are you called to fire departments?"

"I like to wander. They don't usually task me with specific places or areas."

"Something we can agree on."

"We seem to agree on most things."

"Maybe I'm just buttering you up."

"Going to toast me?"

Haven paused and let out a laugh. "Clever joke, honey, but I'm not the fiery type."

"These mortals definitely are." Airen gestured toward the people in front of them frantically trying to put out the flames.

"It's not that bad, they'll get the hang of it."

"I kind of thought they would make places like this fireproof, you know?"

"They can't think of everything."

"Perhaps we should influence more protective architecture."

"They'll learn to do it themselves after this."

"Maybe. Not all humans are the brightest."

"True."

The pair watched an energetic young man run back and forth, spraying the fire hose around the truck. "Wow!"

he yelled. "That was fast, I didn't even know those things were combustible, you know? Look at that, those flames are so orange its crazy. I really fucked this up, huh?"

A tall, muscular woman stood next to him. "No more opening suspiciously old containers, Rodney...especially during controlled fire training!"

"My bad, my bad. At least we know the stuff is flammable, and what better training than this?"

"I'm making you re-paint the truck."

"Fair enough."

Haven smiled. "At least he's honest."

"He is right, this is good training," Airen agreed.

Haven's eyes wandered to the side of the building. "What the fuck?"

"What?"

Its light grey form stood out against the building. Its surface waved with the breeze, refusing to lose shape even as the thick smoke morphed through its form, dissipating into clean, clear air.

"What is it doing?" Airen asked. "Illfell aren't supposed to wander the Mortal Realm."

"I don't know."

"That's weird... Is it purifying the air?"

"There isn't any research on these things in the Mortal Realm. We don't know what they are capable of here."

"We don't know what they are capable of anywhere, they just linger and reach out menacingly... What should we do about it?" Airen asked.

"I'm not sure. We should at least watch it for a while, see what it does."

"Where did the shuck go?"

Haven looked around. "I...don't know."

"I'm surprised Luck didn't destroy the thing. Perhaps it was headed elsewhere?"

"Yeah, probably." *I don't like this... It's a little too strange...too many odd things all at one spot.*

"Do you think they know what they are looking at?"

"This one seems to, its staring right at us."

"I wonder why."

Its figure began to fade, dispersing into the air with the last of the smoke. The hoses stopped. The clambering footsteps stilled. Even the wind dyed down.

"Creepy..." Haven said.

"Yeah..." Airen turned back toward the people. "Seems they got the fire under control."

Rodney stood inside, staring at the truck. "It's not too bad, not at all. I can get it clean."

The taller woman shook her head. "Any damage?"

"A little on the hood, and that window is broken, also this latch is melted. Won't be getting into there anytime soon."

She sighed. "Grab Bobby and get it fixed up."

"Bobby!" Rodney ran up to a younger man with scruffy blonde hair, sitting in a chair. "You awake? Come on, I know you love sleep, but I would have thought the building catching fire would have woken you up at least a little."

The man stretched and opened his eyes. "My brothers used to catch things on fire for fun."

"Give me a hand, will you? Dina wants us to fix up the engine."

"O..."

"Let's go." Rodney grabbed his arm and dragged him toward the front.

"K..."

"Where's the paint? I guess we should call someone about the window, maybe grab the toolbox."

"Right," Bobby said, working on the melted latch.

"Did you know that box was flammable? I mean, no one told me what was in it. It might have had Sharpie writing on it that said, 'Rodney don't touch,' but, you know, I can't not touch something that clearly states I can't. You know me, Dina knows me, even Mo knows better. Someone was asking for trouble, I think."

"Sure, Rodney."

"Fun group," Haven said. "We should people-watch here more often."

"We should," Airen agreed. "I guess we weren't needed. Not sure why the shuck led us here."

"Maybe just in case they couldn't get it under control."

"Maybe. What should we do now? The illfell vanished in a very mysterious manner."

"Well, if you feel you've had enough excitement for one day, you could always come by my place and have some tea. I could use a break."

Airen smiled. "I'd love to. Where do you live?"

Haven opened a portal and offered her hand, leading Airen to an older cabin in the Omen Lands with a simple grey wooden door. "Not sure what this was built for. It's kept up over the years."

"It's nice. When did you move out of the Underrealm?"

"I never really lived there. Found this place pretty early on and liked the privacy. Not much of that down there."

"Not much in the Halo either."

The interior was just as gloomy as the surrounding landscape. Every board, every chair, every piece of fabric, even the windows were tinted a slight grey.

Airen stepped closer to a bookshelf. "A single color—as lonely as it is down here, this is where it shows its true vibrance. So many shades and tones, so many differences. To think, if you were only allowed to see one color, it would seem so lively and vast, all because you knew nothing else. Even though I can see more, I still admire its depth."

"You do have a wild eye for detail, enough to get philosophical about a color, one that not all humans even count as a color."

"It's just as different as the rest of the colors. I don't think it should be dismissed."

43

"Even our kinds argue over that. Mostly because of what happened here. This place turning grey was interpreted as it losing all color."

"I don't see it that way. It simply diminished into one."

"For what purpose?"

"Perhaps to teach us the value of each color. They weren't all needed here to show its importance."

Haven stepped closer, gently pulling Airen's chin toward her. "If only others had such beautiful eyes, maybe they could see more like you." *Did that make her blush? Cute.*

"What do yours see?"

"My new favorite color."

She... I... That's sweet...

Haven stepped back toward the kitchen. *Well, wasn't hard getting her all flustered.* She grabbed a modern kettle, filling it with water.

"Do you have power here?"

"No, Ginner made a power source for me using pieces. What kind of tea do you want?"

"What do you have?"

"Some ginger-based flavors, mint, high caffeine, herbal blend, and cinnamon."

"Mint." She sat at a small table, watching Haven prepare the mugs. "I didn't know pieces still worked here."

"They were originally made to help fallen or those with broken staffs to regain power or status, so they were made to work in every realm. Now most magical beings carry

44

them. Some are paranoid about losing their abilities, others just want to feel powerful." She pulled a bright green rhombus-shaped energy stone from her pocket. "They still keep their colors as long as they don't touch the ground."

"Interesting."

"Here." Haven handed her a mug and sat beside her. "Ever use a piece? Can't imagine you would need to with that divine staff of yours."

"I haven't. How do they work?"

"Just hold it in your hand and think of a curse or blessing. The magic will follow your instructions just as well as a staff would, though a piece is only good for one act."

Airen's eyes focused on Haven's face, her calm grey eyes and soft expression. *I would like to bring it up again... Perhaps ask why she keeps trying to fluster me.*

"What's that contemplative look for?"

"I'm...interested in you."

"In what way?" Haven asked with a playful grin. "Feeling like breaking a few rules?"

"Are there any rules about keeping our kinds separate?"

"No, it's just normal."

"Has it always been, even back when the original eighteen were cast?"

"I guess not. They say the originals used to work together. They like to talk about reflecting each other's work."

"Yes, Gabriel speaks that way. He respects demons just as much as he respects the other archangels."

"Most of the archdemons are of similar mindset, at least that I've heard. Even the most destructive tend to have some boundaries when dealing with an opposing being."

"You seem interested in pushing boundaries."

"And you have yet to push me away." Haven moved closer to her. "Perhaps you want to push them as well."

"Perhaps." Airen leaned against her and closed her eyes. *If only we could all be this peaceful.*

She's cute... Wonder what she's feeling. Haven glanced out of the window. Small, dark drops fell slowly from the air outside. "You were right. It is still beautiful. As still as it is, the rain still falls on the rare occasion."

"I thought the Omen Lands were unmoving?"

"Usually is, but having both of us and several pieces in this cabin is causing mild disturbances. If you give this place enough energy, it will move ever so slightly. It isn't the first time I've seen it rain. It can fall in any direction here."

"Did it used to do that when it was an active realm?"

"Yes, all the weather, the streams, the winds, even the creatures could move in any direction. There was no need for a specific up or down. The gods could move everything as they pleased."

"Even after they are gone, their world still defies rule."

"It always will."

Chapter 7
Among the Branches

"It's there...right there! I swear I saw it move."

"It's just the wind, Dalton." The nurse grabbed his arm and slowly helped him back to his room.

His feet shuffled unevenly across the floor. His mind raced, analyzing the image over and over again, distorting the tree. He could feel its roots shifting into his mind, twisting around his comforts, suffocating his logic. His eyes stared down at the green tiles beneath his feet. *It was there... I must warn the others...stay away from the trees. Stay away from the trees.*

The door closed. The nurse took a deep breath. *Please, let them sleep tonight.* The lights shut off, allowing the dim, clouded evening sky to fill the hallway.

Airen walked up to the window. A small branching omen stared back at her. Its limbs twisted into the tree, blending in almost perfectly. *Out of all the omens, these scare mortals the most. Twisting through the trees, unseen by those who are too distracted, too focused on their lives. The ones who lean into madness, who see shadows of their sins, will count the branches, straining their eyes to watch for movement.* "One that was once a piece of a god, how you cause fear in them..."

"Perhaps it's because they take the form of a familiar thing." Haven joined her. "Something that's normally still and harmless, seeing its branches twist unnaturally, the feeling that something is staring back at them. It's unnerving to mortals."

"The omens that do not hide from them are also the ones most rarely seen."

"Mortals were far more afraid of the god that made these guys. Suddenly seeing a massive, skinny tree fluctuate, they can't even tell the normal branches from the god's parts. The look in mortal eyes, absolute terror."

"I don't know, mortals seem equally scared of the water omens."

"People are easily scared of the ocean in general. Besides, the water omens can sometimes pass as weird squids."

"True. Are you here for a task?" Airen asked.

"I help maintain the madness here. Can't have everyone improve so easily. Ginner's usually here as well, but he's busy trying to clone himself again, so I'm solo today. Who or what are you here for?"

"Gabriel encouraged me to visit some places of struggle to observe functions and prayers. This is one of the more unstable mental institutions." She glared playfully.

"Guilty."

"What sort of things do you typically do?"

"Ginner and I like to play shadows, run around the halls at night to scare the ones that don't sleep. He'll sometimes curse them to see or hear things. The more they go through here, the better life feels to them when they get to return home."

"I guess that's true." Airen watched the doors and listened to the sounds of struggle. Whispers of madness, fear, anger, and confusion. The rare few slept peacefully in their beds, those that were close to recovery and those allowed pills to silence their minds.

"Feeling sad?"

"Yes... I knew a man that had to come to a place like this back when I was alive. He was one of the kindest people, but his parents had brought him too much pain. He became paranoid and started hearing things."

"That uncle of yours that thought gargoyles were watching him?"

"Yes. I was never allowed to visit him. My family didn't want me to see such a place."

"Too bad, the ones that do better usually have regular visitors. Having someone from the outside world that still cares and is willing to help you through it makes it much easier."

"Perhaps I shall encourage more to visit their maddened friends, then." Airen smiled. "To think, I'm getting good ideas from a demon."

"Well, we are, at the end of the day, here for the same reason: to help humanity thrive through hardships and happiness."

Yelling and crying emerged from a nearby room. Her words were sporadic, flying out of her mouth in incoherent ramblings. "Guns in my head. Guns in my head!" The voice repeated over and over, growing in volume.

Airen lifted her divine staff and looked at Haven. "Are you going to stop me?"

"No, she's been tormented enough."

The staff glowed brightly. The woman's cries began to quiet, returning the soft ambiance to the air. Their ears once again filled with the gentle sounds of pens on paper, soft feather dusters, and brooms along the floor.

"Probably the most peaceful this place has ever been," Haven said.

"Does that bother you?"

"No. I have something more important going on tonight anyways." She stood up. "Come on, we have a dinner to go to."

"Dejen's?"

"He invited me over this evening, so I thought I'd hijack you for a while."

Airen took her hand and followed her through a portal, reappearing in front of a small door in a cramped alleyway. The bricks were covered in paintings and chalk designs of all sorts.

"Dejen encourages the community members to liven up the walls," Haven said. "He made friends with all the cops, so they don't get in trouble."

"You're right, he would make a good angel."

The door swung open. "Ah, Haven and Airen, just in time, come in, come in." The house was lively with chattering children, small cats, and colorful decorations. Dejen sat at the dining table. "Mia, they've arrived."

A shorter woman with puffy, dark hair and a tie-dye cooking apron walked in. "Wonderful, it's great to meet you." She smiled at Airen. "Dejen is always inviting people over. He has an eye for the interesting folks."

Haven nudged Airen's side. "Couldn't get more interesting than us."

Mia set a large bowl onto the table. "The kids have friends over, so they won't be pestering us tonight." She sat next to her husband. "Seafood stir fry, and there is hot water in the kettle if you'd like some tea. I made sure to get more of your favorite, Haven. Has she tried it yet?"

"I haven't." Airen responded.

Haven poured them both a mug. "It's got a kick to it."

Airen took a sip, immediately met with the strong taste of cinnamon. "Yes...it does."

"Stronger than a cup of coffee," Dejen agreed.

"So," Mia started, scooping food into her bowl. "How did you two find each other?"

Haven spoke. "Found her wandering around, tending to strays. Wasn't used to seeing other people around, so I decided to be social."

"Do you live together?"

"Not yet." Haven winked.

Airen smiled. "Feeling lonely?"

"Perhaps. I wouldn't mind having you around more often. You can help me keep Scraps out of trouble."

Airen watched Scraps dart around the room, playing with the cats. *Animals can see omens... I'll have to ask Haven about that later.* A small brown cat jumped into her lap and curled up for a nap.

Haven reached over to pet the animal. "Really, Chip, you're not even going to say hi to me first? I used to be your favorite."

"Airen is wearing softer clothing," Dejen said.

She gestured toward her black and red jacket. "At least I have more variety."

"Fair enough, though the soft colors suit her."

"Thank you," Airen responded. "I do wear darker colors on special occasions."

Dejen grabbed his colorful robe covered in leaves and birds. "I prefer comfort and variety."

Haven smiled. "You do have an unreasonable amount of those things. Rarely see you in the same robe twice."

"My wife makes them. She's an exceptionally skilled seamstress. The robes I wear are used as tests to make sure the design holds and washes well. They are then donated to homeless shelters so even the poor can have a variety of lively cloths."

"Each day is unique," Mia said. "I like to encourage that as much as I can."

Airen smiled. *They would both make good angels. I wonder if the Lord knows of them.*

It wasn't a rarity, not odd at all for people to sit around a table and chat the evening away, even with nine cats, four children, and lingering omens. The oddity was plainly in sight causing laughter and teasing remarks.

Dejen smiled. "Are you sure you're not an angel as well, Haven? It would fit you better, especially your name."

"I'm certain. I don't do terrible things on my time off, but I can be a bitch."

"I have yet to see it," Airen added.

"Ha," Dejen laughed. "Perhaps Airen is raising you up, redeeming you slowly."

"That's not how it works. Even as divine as she is, she cannot remove the color from my wings."

"Doubting my grace?" Airen asked.

"You may be powerful enough to have that pretty white hair of yours, but even you can't switch a demon."

Dejen raised a glass. "To the most respectable demon I know."

"Chatting with others?"

"Who knows, most people don't tell you who they really are. I could be chatting with dozens, and I'd be oblivious."

"Ok, fair."

Dejen looked up at a colorfully painted grandfather clock. "Four hours. You are far too great company." He stood. "We will be getting the children to bed soon."

"Good luck with that," Haven said.

"I have some candles for you in the shop in a green bag."

"Thanks."

"We'll meet you at the door." He turned toward Airen. "So wonderful to have your company. She found a good one."

I noticed she didn't correct him either. We aren't together, but the idea is nice. "Thank you. Glad to know she has good friends. She did seem a bit solitary when we first met."

"She has been coming around for a few years now. Always has something interesting to talk about. Even the local priest is suspicious of her with how much she jokes about being a demon."

"Do you believe her?"

He stopped on the porch. "I know you aren't normal. For someone like me, raised between the physical and the spiritual, it is not hard to see. You both have great energy. How you got it is your business. You will always be welcome as friends, even if you are divine beings."

"Thank you. It is rare to find people so open-minded."

"Is it just as rare among angels?"

"Less so, though all beings, mortal or not, have their own differences and personalities."

He smiled. "That is what I cherish. Without difference, there would be no adventure, no purpose. I will always welcome anyone into my home no matter who or what they are."

Haven walked out. "And that's why your place is the best for people-watching." She grabbed Airen's hand. "Thanks for the candles. See you around, Dejen."

He even thought she was odd for a demon. Perhaps all of our perspectives are skewed in some way. The omens probably have the best understanding of us. They have no pull to either side, no mortal teachings to sway them. Perhaps they are the ultimate outer perspective. She stared down at Scraps.

"What is it, Airen? You look like you have a question."

"Can animals always see omens, or do they have to show themselves?"

"They have to show themselves, though they don't seem to hide from animals as much as people. Most animals don't mind them."

"Scraps was keeping the cats entertained. I wonder if they can communicate with each other."

"We'll probably never know," Haven said.

"I guess that's why so many people aren't made into after-beings. Humans are far too curious to accept the unknown as it is."

"That's what makes Dejen so likeable. He isn't drawn to the same self-destructive flaws. Hell, he practically already has the mindset of an angel. Wouldn't need any training, just toss him a staff and tell him to have fun."

"He would love the clothing perks. Magical cloth cleans itself and can be any array of colors. I'm sure he would still wear a new pattern every day."

"No doubt."

"Then you would have more angels to have tea with."

"Might need to bring more demons in to balance out our mix."

"People would greatly benefit if those two were made angels." Airen moved closer and tightened her grip. "Though something tells me they would if you were one too."

Chapter 8
Clovers

The trees were filled with omens, twisted branches with hollow, grey eyes. Eyes that they couldn't see. No matter how hard mortals studied the trees, climbed their structures, no matter how many photos they took, they would never see the eyes of moving branches.

I wonder if they speak to each other, Airen thought, staring out of a small window. *Perhaps each type has its own form of communication, or maybe all omens can understand one another. I wonder if they will ever speak, if they change at some point, become more or less or just different than what they are now.* She could see their eyes glowing with energy, never blinking or closing, never shifting or changing. *Can they see colors?*

She turned her head away from the window, noticing the sound of strained breathing, the scent of blood, the feeling of impending loss. She stepped down the hall, peeking into a dimly lit cell. A man laid on the floor, shivering in pain. His eyes were bloodied and bruised. His right leg shattered.

"You spoke one too many words, old man," Haven said, appearing next to him.

"I have been judged by my kind." Tears fell from his eyes, mixing with his blood. He strained to cough. "They...aren't helping me..." He reached toward the bars, barely able to see.

"No." She grabbed his hand, encouraging him to lay his head back down.

"It hurts..."

"I know. It will fade."

"Will I become one of you?"

"That is for the Lord to decide." She tightened her grip on his hand.

"Thank you, Haven. I would have been alone." He coughed once more and handed her a small white clover. His eyes closed. His lungs ceased. His hands succumbed to the cold. The room filled with silence, though Haven's mind was filled with sound. An old song, she didn't know from where. A calming melody of death, soothing those that were falling into its grasp. Haven could see the hollow eyes of thousands, bodies laid upon the ground, soaking the rocks beneath in blood. A vision that followed her to every death, every last breath she witnessed. She would always remember them.

Airen stepped out of the shadows and sat next to the two. "You put him out of his misery."

"No fun toying with dying souls."

"You never hurt him, only reminded him of his wrongs."

"Didn't see a point." Haven closed her eyes. She had grown fond of chatting with him, a broken man that was shoved from grace. An odd feeling of understanding always lingered in the back of her mind.

"You feel sorrow for him."

"No one deserves to suffer like that."

"May I ask about the clover?"

"He had a daughter. She gave it to him for good luck. They used to visit him, stopped about...twenty years ago. Just got too busy, didn't see a point in visiting a broken man in an endless cage."

She cares for him, for them. Airen's eyes filled with warm admiration. Her emotions shifted. "To be honest, I would be grateful to have you watching over me as a human."

"You'd prefer a demon?"

"I'd prefer you."

"What kind of trouble do you think your divine ass would get into?"

"I don't know, but if I were to deserve it, I would gladly welcome your shadows." Airen leaned against her, allowing her wing to rest against Haven's back.

A shadowed omen touched the man's head. Its body shook and strained, radiating strange pulses of energy. Its form glitched between stone and shadow, glowing with a dark presence.

Haven's eyes widened. "Scraps?"

"What's wrong with him?" Airen asked.

60

"I don't know. Haven't seen him do that before." She reached toward him. "Come here, let's see you." He leapt onto her lap, curling up with strained movements. "His energy is unstable. Might have something to do with his uncurable fractures."

Airen reached out to rest her hand on his back. The omen's movements calmed. His form returned to solid stone. "There you go. Hope that feels better." She looked up into Haven's eyes. "Wouldn't want you losing two friends in one night."

Haven put an arm around her. "Thanks, Airen."

Chapter 9
Blue Silk

Soft blue fabric rested against her skin. Darker, circular patterns lined the bottom edge and sleeves, matching her shoes. Below her were glowing pools of light blue. The floor moved with each step, waving around like cool ocean waters, though its surface was smooth and firm to the touch.

"Magnificent, isn't it?" Gabriel asked, walking in wearing a deep green robe with golden accents. His long beard was tied with golden ribbons.

"Yes," Airen responded. "I'm sure Galea is spending her every breath bragging about it."

"No one is more serious about the bonds of magic and structure. Everything has energy, a life of its own."

I wonder if the Underrealm has a place like this.

"Speaking of," Gabriel continued, "I should help Greg out. She's been talking his ear off for long enough."

"Good luck." Her eyes wandered across the room. Soft white wings filled the air. Each pair was accompanied by different colors, styles, shapes, and forms. *This is what they want, right? A peaceful place to be accepted no matter what. Who you are, where you came from, what you look or* sound like. *We are happy here. Is this what mortals want as well?* She smiled. *I'm sure Dejen would love this.*

She focused her attention onto their eyes. The newest angels had theirs wide with awe and uncertainty, still learning the ways of finalized harmony. Each moment slowly drained their suspicions and cautions as they gave into the gaze of those more content. The eldest were gathered in the back, laughing with confidence. Most of their eyes were filled with happiness and excitement, the thrill of a dance with no drama or ill intent. *So many eyes glazed with wonder. A shame that look is so rare among mortals.*

Her hand reached for the door, slowly revealing the warm breeze of the clouds. The sun was slowly setting behind the white horizon.

"Hey, gorgeous."

Her eyes darted toward the border. "Haven? Lingering in shadows today?"

"Heard the Halo was having a celebration. Thought I'd get a glance at the action."

"Spying on me again?"

"Better me than one of the creeps that usually stalks around here." She pulled a glowing orange piece out of her pocket. "Paid the guy at the border to walk away for a bit. The newest ones never know what to do."

"I think his name is Greg. Izeah told me about him. He is a bit clueless."

"Makes my life easier."

"I assume you have dance halls in the Underrealm as well?"

"Yes. Most of the parties held there are suit-and-tie type. All the archdemons and higher-ups gather to chat and pretend they are above everyone. Not all that different from mortal business parties, if you think about it."

"And here I though your kind would be the more wild type."

"We are, just not at those parties."

"Do you attend them?"

"No... I'm not really the type."

"Would you rather attend one of ours? I'd take you if it was allowed."

"I'm sure that would go well with your friends. Bringing a demon to a party would liven things up."

"Perhaps I'll take you to one in the Mortal Realm."

"Asking me out, Airen?"

"Perhaps." Airen turned toward the large doors. "Looks like more are coming out to enjoy the air."

"Why don't we go for a walk before I get you into trouble?" Haven grabbed her hand and led her through a portal.

"Where are we?"

"Brannen St. Café."

"Are we here for conversation or a date?"

"Maybe a date, or maybe I just like this place. They have killer pies." Haven led her toward a tall table in the corner. "Bet it's better food than they were serving at the party."

"Have you tried Duke's cooking before? Nothing beats it."

"Sure, an angel has an advantage, but for simple, magicless food, noting beats this place."

"I'll have to try it, then. How has your day been?"

"Had to chase a new demon around. They were far too excited about their abilities, and the demon tasked to them couldn't keep up."

"You had an exciting day."

"So did you."

"I wish mortals could have times like those. The Halo parties are so peaceful and accepting. Mortals are always having to bend to social norms just to attend." She stirred her tea with a saddened expression.

"What's wrong, honey?"

"We...haven't really made it much better. Humans improve for a while, then fall back into old, controlling habits. It just seems tiring trying to keep up with the waves of acceptance versus judgement. I don't always feel like we make enough of a difference."

Haven grabbed her hand. "They do fall back sometimes, and I know my kind are often to blame, but they need to learn. One day they will. One day they'll look back at how repetitive their history has been and say, 'Enough.' Most intelligent mortal species like ours function like this. They just need time to grow."

Airen looked up with a raised eyebrow. "How do you know about other species?"

Haven's expression went blank. The sentence repeated in her head in a soft, calm tone. *Most intelligent mortal species like yours function like this, they just need to grow.* "I...think the Lord said it once."

"To you?"

"I haven't met them. I probably overheard them say it."

"Do you know what they look like?"

Her mind flashed with a tall figure bathed in colors and light. "Vaguely... Have you met them?"

"Yes, a few days after I was cast. They came to visit and discuss progress with the archangels. Izeah was happy to have me tag along."

"As pretty and intelligent as you are, I'd take you with me to boring meetings too."

"They aren't usually boring. The Lord is rather captivating."

"I'd still be staring at you." *She's blushing again.*

Scraps leapt onto the table, knocking over Haven's tea. "Really?" Haven glared at him. He reached for her arm, gesturing for her to follow. "Going to interrupt us now?" The omen shook his head and ran out the door. "Alright, let me at least get our pies first."

-

Scraps darted through a tall metal gate. The sky shifted with warm colors reflecting over shining stones and waving flowers. Each blade of grass was trimmed, each bush was well cared for, allowing the brightest collection of flower petals to drift through the air, leaving dots of warmth among the field.

"How often do you visit places like this?" Haven asked.

"Occasionally," Airen responded. "I've visited family, helped a few mortals though hard times. You?"

"Not my favorite place to be."

"Any particular reason?"

Haven's mind filled with images of blood-soaked swords, old-fashioned graves, and lifeless eyes. "Just...an old nightmare."

Airen turned toward a gravestone surrounded by pale blades of grass. A soft light grey illfell stood in front of it, staring down at the name.

Haven watched as Scraps wandered around the creature, refusing to go near. "You aren't going to attack it either, huh? Is that the same one from the fire station?"

"It seems to be. I haven't seen any others in this realm." Airen took a few steps closer. "Whose grave is that?"

It had a smooth marble surface, orange in color. Clean and bright compared to the dull, faded ones around it.

Joe Varenfield

"The kindest of things can often be found behind the darkest of wings."

Haven glared at the clouded figure. "Why here, huh?" The creature didn't react, no sound or movement, as if all it could see was the grave before it. Haven sat down at a nearby bench and pulled out the clover. "Just like the omens, you'll never tell us."

Airen sat next to her. "I believe the quote was about you."

"He never saw my wings."

"No, but he knew you were a demon."

"I wonder if they came to visit him."

"His family?" Airen asked.

"They didn't think it was worth it to keep visiting him when he was alive."

"They'll need closure too. Even if they don't, we're here for him."

Haven smiled and leaned against her. "What is it about this cloud...?"

What does it see? Airen wondered, gently rubbing her thumb across Haven's hand. *Is it staring at the name, the grave itself, or even the man below? Why him? Why Joe?*

The sunset brought vast, warm colors to the illfell's form, matching the clouds above. It remained for thirty minutes, swaying with the breeze until it dissipated, returning to the invisibility of the evening air.

-

The dim evening covered the Halo in a blanket of calm resonance. Some were still trickling out of the dance hall, readying for rest. Others were stepping out to watch the brightening of the stars.

"Wandered off again?" Gabriel asked.

"Wanted to go for a walk." Airen responded.

"You were gone for some time."

"I ran into a friend. She needed some company."

"Probably better. I, unfortunately, spent most of the evening listening to Galea. Some of the newer angels were curious about design. She kept bringing me into the conversation, telling her favorite stories about our trials with the godly beasts."

"She does like to tell tales. I'm sorry I wasn't able to rescue you from it."

"Where did you go?"

"The Mortal Realm. My friend wanted to take me to a café, though we ended up getting interrupted by an omen."

"What sort?"

"Gargoyle."

"Causing mischief?"

"No, it led us to something...odd."

"What?"

"An illfell wandering around the Mortal Realm. It wasn't the first time we'd seen it."

"Really?" Gabriel asked. "I didn't think them capable. They always gather around our borders."

"Perhaps it's because of how we have been dealing with them lately?"

"Perhaps. I wonder if they will end up affecting the mortals in any way. Could you continue to monitor this creature?"

"Of course."

Loud chatter echoed between the buildings. Galea stepped around the corner with a tall glass of wine. "Gabriel, Airen, leaving already?"

"Yes," Gabriel responded. "We were, um..."

Airen took his arm. "We were going to head to the library to do some illfell research."

Galea smiled. "Sounds exciting."

"Yes, have you told the new ones about the library yet?"

"No, I haven't." She turned toward a group of young angels. Their eyes widened with panic.

Sorry. Gabriel mouthed before quickly walking away.

Chapter 10
Red Candles

The Underrealm was no stranger to the sun. Their dark stone structures and red-hazed atmosphere were just as lively throughout the day as they were in the moon's presence. Even their gates shined with vast colors in the rays of light, though instead of gold, their gates were made of solid black obsidian with rust-colored accents. Instead of white clouds and marble, there was smoke and black stone.

The buildings stood as grand and tall as those above. Architecture made with equal passion, rising a silent battle between twins. Each building found its own unique face, a power few could truly admire. Some bore fresh smooth surfaces, while others were cracked and faded, showing the years of wear from the hands of magical beings. Even the oldest of cobblestone structures were respected as a welcome sight of home.

Glasses clanked across the room. Red webbed wings and bright, burning eyes blended into the smokey atmosphere. The rough brick walls were covered in old weapons, flickering candles, and gruesome paintings made from human blood. The old chairs and tables were constantly collecting ash and dust on their surface. Few cared enough to try and keep them clean. One wave of their wings was usually enough for those with shifting eyes and greedy ears more focused on laughter and schemes. It was familiar. She had decades of regular attendance, listening to stories, rumors, and underhand job offerings. Even still, she always felt out of place. Haven shrugged off the ever-looming feeling as she reached behind the bar and grabbed a bottle.

"It'll be easy. She's still pretty new," a demon said, sitting at a nearby table.

"What's her name?" another asked.

"Airen."

"Paid?"

"Paid."

"How much?"

The man tossed a small, rhombus-shaped piece on the table, glowing bright blue. "Ten pieces."

"Who charged it?" Haven asked, turning toward them.

"I don't know. I wasn't all that sober when I spoke with them earlier today. They did give us potential locations and everything. Wanted it done quick."

"Airen, you said?"

"Yes. We don't know much about her. You interested?"

"I'll take care of it. It's been a while since I've witnessed a fall."

He tossed her the small pouch of pieces. "Let us know how it goes."

"Every gruesome detail, preferably," one added, curling his fingers into the table.

"We'll see." She set the bottle down and turned toward the door with a grin. *Might want to keep it to myself. They aren't going to expect this... Now where is she?*

-

Airen stepped out and took a deep breath. Her simple blue and white floral dress swayed in a warm breeze. The sounds of laughter and gossip battered against the door, trying hard to reach her ears.

"An angel by a church, what a sight."

"Haven, are you tending to a job?"

"I thought I'd tend to you for a while."

"Feeling social?"

"Perhaps."

Airen stepped closer. "Have an interesting day?"

"The usual jobs, nothing out of the ordinary. What sort of fun were you getting into?"

"Izeah wanted to take me to a church for a celebration. They get quite lively."

"Right, I forget about the mortal holidays. Did you stay hidden?"

"No, we introduced ourselves as travelers just stopping by for the day."

"Always a good go-to story."

"You seem more regular with the mortals."

"I've watched many lives go by, usually don't stick around for too long," Haven said. "Don't want them getting too attached or suspicious of my inability to age."

"Don't want to break hearts?"

"Not theirs. They have enough to go though as it is. You ever think about it, getting 'close' to a human?"

"No."

"Another angel, then?"

"No." Airen looked away, smiling with a slight blush.

"Perhaps you'd be into something more daring?"

"Perhaps... Have you ever had those desires for another of your kind?"

"No, though I have had some that tried...still do."

"Then I do have competition."

Haven grinned. "Not much. I don't find any of them nearly as interesting or beautiful as you."

Airen smiled. "You don't really sound like a demon."

"Questioning my heinousness?"

"A little."

"Perhaps I do need to break a few more hearts. Want to volunteer?" She nudged Airen's shoulder.

Airen leaned into her. "You don't seem the type to break things."

"I can pick up a few more bad habits. Don't want to be slacking too much."

"I won't shy away from you. Something tells me you're all bark."

"Perhaps you're too trusting."

"Perhaps... If you wouldn't even break a mortal heart, I doubt that you would try to break mine."

"You are a much higher target. I could get a lot of power and respect from breaking you." She winked. Grey eyes met blue, exchanging hints of emotion, intent, and a shared pull of temptation.

A nearby door swung open, spilling out loud, cackling humans onto the sidewalk. The pair stopped and watched the group fumble around in the dark, clueless what direction they were facing.

Haven smiled. "Drunk fools."

"At least they are having fun."

Haven grabbed her hand. "Come on." She stepped through a portal, watching all but grey fade from sight. All signs of life dissipated into stillness.

"Where is your shadow?" Airen asked.

"Probably off running around with the other omens. They like to hang out around humans during celebrations."

"Well, I'd hate to leave you alone." Airen opened the cabin door and stepped inside. "It is nice to have a quiet place to go to."

"It is more enjoyable with you around."

"You don't often have visitors?"

"A couple rarely stop by, don't ever stay. Most of them don't really like the feel here. Too quiet and still."

"Not one to break the stillness with rowdy visitors?"

"As much as I like a good party, I'd rather not have my place destroyed. Demons tend to get wild, though it can be entertaining to watch."

"I find you very entertaining," Airen said.

"Well, you have me all to yourself for now, unless one of your kind is planning a visit."

"Not that I know of. I haven't told anyone about this place."

"No one to save you from whatever nefarious plans I have, huh?"

"Perhaps I like having you to myself."

"Almost sounds like you're planning your own nefarious schemes."

"Something tells me you would like that."

"Depends on what role I play."

Airen stared into her eyes. Haven had seen the look before, though she couldn't place where. The softness that yelled for affection, pleaded to be close, yet still held back enough to keep her still.

Let's see if she'll let me... "Airen, come here."

Airen stepped closer. Her eyes widened as Haven pulled her onto her lap, staring with a confident smile.

"You aren't pulling away." Haven said, wrapping her arms around her.

"I don't feel the need to."

She tightened her grip, pulling Airen closer to place a soft kiss on her lips. She could feel her heartbeat quicken but not race, her breathing stayed calm. No fear or hesitation.

"Why don't we enjoy this evening?"

Airen opened her eyes and leaned her forehead against Haven's, feeling her arms travel across her back. "I enjoy every second with you."

Haven tightened her grip and lifted Airen off the chair, bringing her to the bed. "Wings away, divine."

Chapter 11
The Eyes of Curious Things

Small feet clambered up her body, stopping at her shoulder. Haven let out a sigh and tried to stretch her arm to no avail. *What?* Her eyes were met with soft white hair. Airen was curled up in front of her, holding onto her arm. *Oh.*

The weight on Haven's shoulder shifted. She turned her head toward the omen. "You have a fun night as well?" she whispered. "Thanks for the privacy."

Scraps nodded his head and snuggled up between them. There was no morning sun, nor darkened night. The lands never shifted their tones, never changed with the seasons or cycles that pushed and pulled at the mortal plane. It was easy to get lost in the stillness, no sense of time, no hint of the actions that played out in the other realms.

Airen took a deep breath and stretched her legs. "Haven?"

"Morning, divine."

"How can you tell it's morning? It's always dim here."

"You learn to feel it after a while." She leaned forward, placing a kiss on Airen's cheek.

"Do you know the time as well?"

"No, why, have somewhere to be?"

Airen snuggled closer. "Not particularly."

"Care for some tea to help you wake?"

"Something herbal."

"Ok."

Haven got up and grabbed a mug, filling it with hot water from a nearby kettle. Her eyes followed the small shadows that darted past the windows. *Curious little things. Better not have been spying on us last night.* A round, stubby, uncoordinated little omen bumped into the window, causing her to let out a chuckle. "To think, they were once mighty gods."

"They had their clumsy moments as well." Airen stood up, stretched her arms, and unfurled her wings into the air.

Haven reached out and stroked her soft white feathers. *Well...that's interesting.* "Feeling ok?"

Airen wrapped her arms around Haven and leaned in. "Of course."

"Almost thought your wings would turn."

"I knew they wouldn't."

"Really?"

"I did say I had no reason to shy away from you."

"Were you expecting me to do that?"

"No...not really," Airen said. "Was this planned? Were you hoping to find me and have us end up like this?"

"Possibly... I wasn't sure if you would. It did seem risky, to be honest."

"Were you worried?"

"No, I'll still love you no matter the color of your wings."

"And I love you equally." Airen leaned in for a kiss.

Haven chuckled. "Too bad, I'd feel pretty powerful if I had felled you that easily."

"Is that what you wanted?"

"No, I'm indifferent, to be honest, though technically it was a paid job. Someone wanted you to fall. I decided to take matters into my own hands rather than let some other demon get a hold of you."

Airen looked concerned. "Paid...by who?"

"Not sure. The vile demons mentioned your name, so I told them I'd handle it."

"Well...you handled things rather well," she responded with a teasing smile.

"And you didn't fall."

"It didn't feel wrong. I trust you."

Haven paused. Her eyes stared wide into Airen's. *Shit... I'm the one that fell...in love, at least.*

Airen leaned into Haven, resting her head on her shoulder. "Even though you're a demon, I can't help but to compare you to divinity. You cause disorder and fright but still have the softest touch. You care for the mortals, truly."

"I could never compare to you, divine. My wings were never white."

"You haven't shown them. How would I know?"

"Not really one for flying. Portals do just fine."

"Is that all?"

Haven looked down. "They...hurt to open."

"Did something happen?"

"No... It's just how I was made. It feels wrong to use them."

"Would you show me? Just for a moment. If I can help..."

Sharp burning aches echoed in Haven's mind, sending a chill down her spine. "Not now."

"Ok."

Scraps darted past them and opened the door, doing his best to balance on the handle. "Right," Haven said, "I have to help Ginner with something today." She handed Airen her mug and leaned forward for a kiss. "I'll come find you when I'm done, sound good?"

"Yes."

"Stay out of trouble."

"If you weren't able to fell me, what chance do others have?"

"Fair point. Don't go attracting other demons. I have enough to worry about to add competitors to my list."

-

The art house was one of the taller buildings among the clouds, with those inside encouraged to find their own space for their craft, high or low, on any wall or surface, it mattered not the direction or media. All creativity was pushed to thrive within its structure.

Nothing had changed or shifted. She didn't fear the eyes of others, the dread of secrets or rumors. The Halo would always be a home to her, even as she strayed farther and farther from its light.

"Izeah, may I have a moment?"

He looked down and smiled. "Of course, Airen. What do you need?" He slowly lowered himself back onto the ground and set down his paints.

"I wish to help a demon with an unusual problem."

"What sort?"

"Her wings cause her pain when they open."

"From an injury?"

"She says they had been like that since she was made. Do you have any suggestions?"

"What do they look like?"

"I haven't seen them yet. She was unwilling during our last interaction. The topic was uncomfortable for her."

"Hmm, perhaps I may know of a few potential causes, though I will need to know what they look like in order to know which applies."

"Thank you, I'll ask when I next see her."

"Anything else?"

"How have things been going with the illfell?" Airen asked.

"Your advice was quite efficient. We have had far fewer lingering since we encouraged some omens to wander the border. May I ask if this information happened to come from this demon of yours?"

"Yes."

"Is that why you have been home far less?"

"Yes."

"Interesting." Izeah smiled. "You are far too kind, Airen. Few make friends with demons, especially so quickly."

"They deserve no different treatment for what they are."

Michael stood across the room, staring at the two. *No, I said it to be done... Lying cheats.* A portal opened in front of him. His glowing white wings cut into the shadows of a cramped alleyway. The sun could barely reach between the two buildings, teasing the ground with a single shred of its light. "Cercaius?"

"Michael." The vile demon stepped closer. He had a short stature, covered in scars and fresh burns. His red webbed wings were torn and tattered. His eyes glowed a bright yellow filled with violent energy.

"I asked a task be done."

"And it was."

His tone darkened with frustration. "She did not fall."

Cercaius stepped back, shifting his brow. "Haven took care of it. She's always fooling around with your kind. We assumed she'd have no trouble felling an angel."

83

Michael froze. Panic flooded his mind. *No... Can't be... Haven is...* "Airen's divine...that must be why it didn't work... What did she do, exactly?"

"Probably slept with her, considering you didn't mention any harm, and she's been flirting with her, I assumed..."

Michael rushed out of the alley, reappearing in his office in the Halo. He was surrounded by painted landscapes, experimental potions, and softly glowing candles, though his eyes glanced over them, whirling around the room as he paced. *Perhaps... No, I cannot change course, it must be done... Haven... Haven...* His eyes shot wide, glued to the soft feathered tips of his wings. Their color had begun to fade into a deep grey. *No... I can't... No...*

"Michael?"

He closed his wings and fixed his composure. "Yes?"

Izeah walked into the room. "I haven't seen you much recently. How has your project been going?"

"Oh, the usual waves of accomplishments and frustrations. I might be able to achieve great progress if things go accordingly."

"I'm glad for you."

"Tell me, was I hearing you speak of our illfell with Airen earlier?"

"Yes, you haven't noticed either, I assume. Spending all your time in your study, you really need to get out more."

"Yes..."

"The illfell have been contained. No more twisted clouds lurking at our borders."

"How was it accomplished?" His eyes relaxed as he watched Izeah pour him a mug of tea. Hot steam rose toward his face as he inhaled the sweet scent of vanilla and lavender.

"We discovered that the omens will attack and dismantle them on sight. It's worked rather quickly, though we're still having trouble moving the larger one."

"As unpredictable as they are, the omens know more of the order than even we. They were, after all, once our gods."

"True words, brother." Izeah stared down at his mug. "I remember those days. The colossal beings they once were, commanding the winds, the fires, the lightning. Our rough and ragged world, now far smoother."

"For that, we give thanks to our Lord."

"To our Lord."

"How was this solution discovered?"

"Airen made a friend with a demon. Apparently, they have been using omens to keep illfell out of the Underrealm for a while now."

Haven... "Really?"

"Perhaps we should pay more attention to our reflections. They may have more wisdom to show us."

"Are you sure they would be willing to comply? Friendly conversation is not quite their style, Izeah."

"They aren't all heathens, Michael. They serve an equal purpose to our own."

"They provide more tricks and betrayal than are worth the effort. I would advise Airen to show caution. She is still young."

"Her age does not define her ability to know when she is being tricked. Garrus has been around for centuries and still falls for the most basic human tricks."

"He is too hopeful for his own good."

"She is reasonable. Honestly, one of the brightest minds I've met. I trust her to handle herself just fine around demons."

Just not that one... "Then perhaps you should be cautious. Her wisdom may one day surpass your own."

Izeah chuckled. "I would be glad to know that humanity will be cared for by such an individual."

They will not... Michael's eyes shifted to uncertainty. *I must...it must be done...*

Chapter 12
David

Dark grey feathers were a rare sight. Most of the fallen hid among humans, chasing their habits and woes, though some chose to remain, fighting their exile, clawing their way back to heinousness or grace. There was one who refused to hide his wings, to clamor and argue with those around. He sat by the water, listening for prayers and cries for help. He stared down at the rushing stream. His short black hair reached toward his eyes. He had never cried, even as he fell. His eyes remained still and cold. None were more fierce a protector for those in need. Few fought so bold and true for mortal lives, though his own haunted him beyond the light. Even his grace could not outweigh the pain he once endured.

"David, may I sit with you?"

His piercing blue eyes lifted. "You are always welcome, Airen."

She sat on the ragged stone and glanced at the staff lying next to him. The top was curved like hers, though the other end was sharp and long, showing the shape of the vile. The handle was jagged, mixed with light blues, white, green, and grey. No other wielded such a relic.

"I haven't seen you around as often," he said.

"I've been preoccupied. Distracted by...well, a love interest."

A hint of a smile came over his face. "Fitting for you."

"Not all would think that."

"Are you here for company?"

"Yes, but also a question. Your wings, do they hurt to open? I met a demon who is unwilling to open hers because of pain. I was wondering if such a thing applied to those fallen."

"They don't." He grabbed the odd staff and stared down at its shifting colors. "Some are just made broken."

"Do you know any others with this problem?"

"No. Is this perhaps the lover you spoke of?"

"Yes."

"Haven?"

"You know her?"

"She is no fallen but still another out of place."

"What do you mean?"

"Wait, she'll show you."

Airen smiled and let out a sigh. Her eyes traveled back to the stream, finding comfort in its ever-changing surface. "Perhaps we are meant to change. Everything does. You, Haven, and I don't exactly fit the original patterns for our kind. More and more, we are shifting, just like the mortals themselves, only slower."

"Change is inevitable, even for those of immortal nature."

"Not everyone follows change."

"If everyone did, it would be less important. There would be fewer obstacles to remind us of that. We don't need to be like the river. We can be more like the shifting surface of a lake, slower and better understood."

"Better to not get swept away."

"We will still someday dry out like the gods that once held the world in their hands. One day, we will no longer be needed. Either we will be replaced or destroyed."

He was known for violence and corruption. Untrusted by most of his kind aside from those divine. Few understood the hollow nature of his eyes, the feeling of loss that tainted their vibrant colors and shared the horrors of his past.

Dark yet...calm, Airen thought. "Even the monster they think you to be, the shadow of corrupted grace holds far more content than any angel of white wings."

He smiled. *You are more than divine, Airen.* His eyes stared across the water, focused on a particular point. "Do you see anything unusual across the water?"

"No, do you?"

She doesn't see them. "Colors are meaningless to me. I don't know exactly when they faded, but light will always catch my attention, always be comforting."

"You don't see it as I do. You don't see the greens of the plants dipping into the water. The colors of the stones and dirt beneath its surface... To you, it is no different than the Omen Lands?"

"Yes."

"You don't know what color my eyes are?" Airen asked.

"No."

"They're blue. A little lighter than yours."

"My eyes are still…"

"They remain the same after we are cast, for the most part. I guess the only one whose eyes you see properly are Haven's. They have always been grey."

"Have they?" *Curious… How many things are actually grey? What already belongs to my world?*

Their eyes shifted to the left. A clouded figure slowly formed next to them, staring with unwavering attention given without eyes. Its shape whisked against the edge of the creek.

"Have you seen it before?" Airen asked. "Haven and I have seen it wandering the Mortal Realm."

"I have, though only recently. I was under the impression that they weren't magically strong enough to survive here, though there have been more illfell forming lately."

"Do you know why?"

"Corruption."

"Of us?"

"Yes."

She looked back at the clouded mass. "Haven helped us take care of the ones in the Halo."

"The ones that surround the Underrealm look more menacing."

"How so?"

"They look more like smoke than cloud and have long spine-like protrusions coming out of their head and back."

"More fitting appearance for demons."

"Have you not seen them?"

"No, I've never been to the border of the Underrealm."

He opened a portal. "Here, I can show you. Perhaps knowing both of their forms will help you solve this oddity."

-

"Haven."

"Azazel, done torturing and scheming for the day?"

He smiled and leaned against the side of the building, blending into the shadows with his usual dark copper jacket and black jeans. "Not quite. I heard about your recent...affair... An angel? Not just an angel, but one with white hair. Now that's a challenge. How crafty of you."

"I actually know how to use conversation instead of ripping everything apart at first glance."

"I do my share of planning."

"So, what's the plan this time?"

"How well is she willing to listen to you?" Azazel asked.

"Why?"

"I'm very interested in meeting her, perhaps at the lake..."

"Trying to screw with an angel again?"

"Technically, you're the one doing the screwing..."

"Fuck off."

"I haven't felt an angel's blood on my hands in so long."

"Get your own."

"What? Don't you want to see her fall? You did take the task."

"Who tasked it anyways?" Haven asked. "The vile was drunk when he was given the charge. He doesn't remember who gave it."

"I don't know, probably some scheming archdemon. Doesn't matter, you weren't able to fell her, so I thought I'd help. I'll let you have your fun."

"She's divine, Az. Not easy to fell."

"You have an advantage. What exactly was your plan with her? I'm willing to go along..."

"Get your own."

"But you already have one so near..."

"Fuck off."

"But..."

"Fuck off, Az. She's off-limits. You aren't usually too lazy to go out and do your own work. You can stay out of my affairs." She shoved him toward the wall and headed down the stairs.

Fire burned along a wall of red stones, cracking blue and white. Demons darted around, throwing fire balls and curses, leaving the walls stained with ash and sparks of magic. Their eyes widened at her form, showing caution. They shifted their magic, making sure not to risk her attention. They knew who she was, the demon that could destroy mortals without need of a staff or the opening of her wings. One of rumors.

Wasteful new casts, always getting too excited and throwing their magic around. Can't get a moment to think around here. The stars danced above her, showing their true forms to her sharp grey eyes. *I'd get a better view at the border. Hell of a lot quieter too.* Her feet led her down a stone path that jutted out of the black-clouded ground. Each stone was precisely placed, perfectly even with the rest. *Damnit, Azazel. I'd better keep her away from him... What? Fuck...* "Airen, didn't expect to see you here."

"David brought me to see the Underrealm illfell. He ran off to distract a demon patrolling the border."

"Probably Tim. He's usually out here at this time."

"How did things go with Ginner?"

"Two more clones. At least the damn things are temporary."

"I'd heard rumors floating around the Halo about a cloning demon. They say he's too preoccupied with his studies to be a threat to people."

"Spot on. He's made, what...thirty of those things so far? They've been lasting longer each time. These ones were around for a whole day and a half."

"That's why you took so long to find me? Do you think he'll get successful one day?"

"Maybe, not sure if the Lord will want to intervene."

"They haven't so far?" Airen asked.

"Nope, not a word. Ginner has been left to do as he pleases. What have you been occupying your time with?"

"Talking with David."

"You two would get along."

"I thought he might know something about your wings. He called you another one out of place."

"Yeah... I'm not the most average demon."

"Well, he's not the most average angel. I thought perhaps you might have something in common."

"Aside from feeling like an outcast, not much. We do act more out of place. He's violent and depressing, and I'm too soft for my own good."

"Are you..."

"No, my wings are still red. If they weren't, I wouldn't be allowed in the Underrealm. I haven't fallen, though I did watch David fall."

"How did it happen?" Airen studied her eyes, admiring the emotions, their colors, the depth that they added to every encounter.

"He corrupted. Nothing pushed him or challenged his grace. He opened his eyes into the Halo, and instead of seeing bright colors and hope, he saw dim grey shadows. I'm not sure why the Lord made him an angel. His life left him far more broken than grace could repair."

"Was his staff always like that? Half divine, half vile?"

"Yes. I'm surprised he doesn't have split wings as well."

"He does everything he can to help people."

"Through death. He will take down anything that threatens a mortal, even another. Only the vile are supposed to take those actions. He does not try to change their minds or better their souls. He has taken countless lives. I guess...it was death that truly claimed him."

Grey wings fluttered in the distance. Sparks of magic rose from behind a thick black cloud. Blood splashed against the surface of a brick wall, brightening its colors.

"What?" Haven rushed forward.

David stood in front of a kneeling demon whose arm trembled as his blood escaped him through a large wound on his shoulder. The demon coughed and fell forward. His legs and neck were covered in blood.

"Tim?"

The demon looked up with a tired gaze. "Haven..." His eyes widened with shock. "The...angel...angel!" He reached for his broken staff, breathing heavily.

Haven got in between them. "Tim, don't..."

His staff pulsed against his hand, causing him to scream out in pain. His eyes glowed and bled. He could no longer hear or see. *Pain... Why did she? Why is she helping them? My head...my...*

David lifted his staff, driving a bolt of energy through the demon's chest. Tim slumped to the ground. His eyes closed. His body began to fade into the clouded ground.

The air became more and more unsettled as everything calmed. Airen had seen the death of mortals, the end of several lives, both peaceful and abrupt, though

95

the eyes of immortals held far more fire. Instead of blood and sorrow, the atmosphere was cold and drained. She struggled to look away. Her ears began to ring. Her eyes grew foggy. She could feel Haven gripping her arm and the sound of muffled voices slowly becoming clearer.

"What were you thinking?" Haven said. "She's the only angel anywhere near here."

"You know he would have killed her."

"She's divine. Tim was an injured lesser. Now she's having to deal with the imbalance effects."

"Haven..." Airen stepped closer, resting her head against Haven's shoulder. "Why am I dizzy?"

"David temporarily corrupted the balance. Normally it only affects him, but since you were here and you're far more of an angel, it affected you."

"David..." Airen looked up at him. "Are you ok?"

His eyes shifted toward her. "Yes."

Even as bright as your eyes are, they still hold such a hollow look. You truly have no eyes for life...

"What the hell happened?" Haven asked him. "Why were you fighting?"

David closed his bloodied wings. "He was tasked to hunt fallen."

Haven let out a sigh. "You ok, Airen? Look at me."

"Yes..."

She's shaking a little... "Let's get you out of here before another demon shows up." Her eyes moved toward David. "You too."

"Yes." He slowly walked through a portal, disappearing from the dark, clouded air.

"Come on, honey." Haven pulled her through a portal, sitting her down on the bed. "You aren't used to watching us fight like that, huh?"

"No."

"Have you ever seen another after-being perish?"

"No... It felt different... Mortals fade and..."

"I know. We aren't really meant to slay each other. Disrupts the balance. That's why you feel strange."

"I'm ok now."

"You sure?"

"Yes. Is that why we never fight in greater numbers?"

"The Lord didn't want us undoing their work, so we were made to feel the balance of energy. A full-on war would leave twice more casualties than desired, so we never cross that line. You're divine, so you should recover quickly. Any normal angel might have blacked out."

"That's why our kinds fight in pairs?"

"So the energy can be shared if one is slain." Haven sat next to her and kissed her forehead. "David's attacked fairly regularly. His...demeanor about death unsettles most."

"I'm not afraid of him."

"Neither am I."

"Did you see it too, his eyes?"

"The fact that they never show emotion, like a deep blue void of death and stillness."

"Yes… Do you know what happened to him? I know he had a difficult life as a mortal."

"I don't. He never talks about it. Lillith claims to know—granted, she claims to know everything."

"What could have made a mortal become something like that?"

"I don't know. Maybe he'll tell you one day. You are good at talking to strange things."

"And you are good at leading me to them."

Haven smiled. "Why don't you lie down for a bit? Let your energy recuperate."

Chapter 13
Stone Eyes

White wings shifted in front of a tall grey statue of a human figure with the head of a black dog. Long, extravagant robes once made of the finest blue and golden silk draped down their body. Their eyes were once shining white surrounded by golden markings that trailed up their long, pointed ears.

"Do you know their name?" Airen asked.

Haven stepped next to her. "Anubis was one. Humans used to believe that they were tasked, that each god had a specific job. The god of death, of the afterlife. They had no true restrictions, just their own goals and ambitions."

"You know more about this place than anyone else I've spoken to, even the angels that studied it. Granted, you do live here."

Haven looked down and closed her eyes. "I...awoke here."

"What?"

"I never saw the gates, the red glare of the bestial bats that guard them, or the waiting eyes of introductory demons."

"Do you remember who you were before?"

"No, no mortal memories. Well, not functioning ones, anyways."

"You...are you sure you're a demon?"

"What else would I be? I have red wings and can go into the Underrealm."

"I don't know...you can't have been made from this realm. Your form has color. Perhaps you were made in the Underrealm but didn't wake right away? I don't know why you would have been brought here, though..."

"Maybe one of the archdemons wanted to mess with me. That doesn't explain everything, though... My wings are still..."

"Maybe they tried to make you fall before you woke?"

"Maybe. I don't have a proper staff—maybe they broke it to see what would happen."

Airen grabbed her hand. "It's sad to think that someone might have tried harming you before you had a chance to take your first steps as an after-being."

"Maybe I'm just an experiment. A demon that wasn't made with a staff."

"You still wouldn't wake here...and the Lord wouldn't have just left you without answers."

Their eyes moved toward the statue. Behind it was a tall, triangular temple, crumbling in the still air. All the statues and structures in the lands had become colorless and grey, though Haven could still picture their hues as clear as day.

Haven spoke. "Anubis preferred to stay as some sort of animal-human hybrid. Most of the gods would keep similar forms in similar areas to be easier to identify, though this particular one was known for shifting their form to confuse mortals. They really liked games."

"So, they were technically all of the Egyptian gods?" Airen asked, following her down a path.

"Yes, and many others across the world."

"Makes me wonder if they kept track of that. How many gods they were to the eyes of mortals."

"Seems like a headache."

"Yeah, especially as populations increased. More stories made about them."

"They are responsible for a hell of a lot of mortal literature. Far more than us."

"Would you want to be in a book?" Airen asked. "You could be one of the stories."

"And have people think I'm a creature with horns and a tail that just likes to torture and seduce people?"

"Still better than people thinking you're a ball of eyes and feathers with wings attached. Why do they think that, anyways?"

"The mortal that wrote the Bible was extremely dramatic. He wanted the angels and demons to seem more distant and unquestionable. Not as human as we really are."

"Just lead to more misunderstandings."

"True. I still like hanging out in the background. They don't need to know about me."

"What about in an after-being book? Then at least it would be more accurate. You might even get more answers if more people know about you."

"I guess, but I'm not about to sit down with one of those snooping storyteller demons for six hours, getting berated with questions about a past I don't even remember."

"Perhaps I could write it. That would give me a perfect excuse to spend more time with you."

"Going to start asking about my hopes and dreams?"

"Perhaps."

"It's not like I can get away from you. You know where I live. You practically live here now too."

"You could always hide from me in the Underrealm."

"And risk you snooping around again?"

"Then you'll just have to give in and answer my unbearable questions."

"Lord, save me."

Airen opened the cabin door, stopping suddenly. "Haven..."

"What's wrong?" She peered in. A shifting, clouded figure stood inside, staring at a bookshelf. "It...it's here now? This thing keeps getting stranger."

"What's it staring at this time?"

"Looks like...Joe's Bible?"

"You kept it?"

"Yeah."

"Why would it be fixated on that?"

"Maybe it was connected to him," Haven suggested. "There are speculations that they form from failed blessings and curses."

"Maybe someone tried to save him from the night he killed those people."

"Maybe."

"How long do you think it will stay?"

"I don't know... Scraps isn't doing anything about it."

"Illfell have never been in the Omen Lands before."

"No, normally they would be destroyed."

"So why is nothing attacking this one?" Airen asked. "The shuck, even Scraps... Noting wants to go near it."

"It doesn't seem all that different from any other illfell, except for its traveling habits."

"Maybe they are changing. Everything does, eventually."

"Now you sound like David."

"He is very philosophical, in a dark way."

"Just don't start acting like him."

"I'm not planning on falling or murdering other afterbeings."

"Good. From what I've seen, it's not pleasant."

The illfell began to fade, whisking out the door, leaving no sound or breeze. Airen sat down. "Where do you suppose it's going now?"

"Wherever it wants, I guess. Doesn't seem all that limited."

"At least it's not hurting anything."

"Not like it can, considering it's made of clouds."

"Good thing clouds aren't deadly to us."

"Would be a hell of a story. Got killed by a menacing-looking cloud."

"It would. A better story, anyways. All the stories of angels and demons being slain are brutal. They are always killed by another after-being or beast..." Airen's smile faded. "Have...you ever killed another after-being?"

"Two. One was a demon that had gone mad and tried going on an angel-killing spree. The other was a fallen demon that..." *Fuck, I don't really want to bring it up...* "He fell after some...questionable things had been done to him by one of the archdemons. He was too far gone to help."

"Can I ask?"

"His name was Arnold."

"Oh... I think I heard about him. The one whose wings were..."

"Yeah... He wouldn't stop screaming."

"You were the one that silenced him." Airen sat next to her and pulled her in for a hug. "I'm sorry, love. I can't imagine what that was like."

Haven closed her eyes. The screaming mixed with the sound of hundreds more. Battle cries, crying horses, clanking metal, and tearing flesh. *Fucking...memories. Why do they keep blurring together? Everything fades back into that same battlefield...*

Airen leaned back. "Izeah told me about Arnold. He admitted that even angels sometimes end up harming each other. We keep just enough of our humanity to still pose occasional threats."

"The Lord didn't want emotionless puppets ruling over people. They wanted them to rule over themselves."

"It does still shock me sometimes. Everything seemed so much nicer when I was cast, but hearing about Arnold and the others that ended like him... We ourselves still have much to learn, and we are just as capable of flaws as the people we once were."

"We still feel what they do."

Airen smiled. "If we didn't, I wouldn't get the chance to love you."

Fuck, that's cute... "You wouldn't get the chance to hate me either."

"This is better than indifference." She leaned forward to kiss her. "If we didn't feel, we wouldn't care to help people. Perhaps we would be more like the omens."

"Doesn't sound too bad, they get into all sorts of fun."

"Not all types of fun..."

"Oh, so you enjoy what we've been getting up to?"

"Perhaps."

Haven pulled Airen on top of her. "Then come here." She watched as Airen's wings shuttered slightly as she placed a soft kiss on her neck. *Cute, they react to her getting flustered. Wonder how they would react to other things... I didn't let her keep them out last time.*

Chapter 14
The Bullish Beast

Warm, soft grass swayed beneath the trees and bright sunlit sky. She had no destination in mind, no task or draw toward any particular direction. She was content wandering the forest, following the paths, and watching the leaves shift and rustle.

How strange... To lose the fear of being lost. I don't remember feeling it too strongly before, but now it's vacant. I can appear anywhere at the blink of an eye no matter where I started. No limitation of my feet or chosen vehicle, no need for maps or paths. I quite enjoy being lost. She turned toward the sound of rustling leaves and high-pitched barks. There was a collection of thick bushes at the bottom of the hill. A tall figure darted around them, reaching for something.

"Get back here... Hey, no throwing sticks at me...smart little thing."

"Haven?"

The figure picked up a small brown puppy and turned toward her. "Airen."

"Who's this?"

"Doesn't have a name yet. I was going to look for a place to drop her off."

"She has no family?"

"Not yet... What?"

Airen grinned. "Not something I would expect from your kind."

"Even we can have soft spots for animals."

Airen reached out to pet the puppy's head. "I think I know a good home."

"Where?"

"Across the street from the park, near the southern edge."

"Ok. You ever had pets?"

"Four dogs. My partner was a softie."

"And you weren't?" Haven teased. The puppy squirmed and wiggled closer to her face. "Cut it out, cutie."

"Have you ever tried to keep one as a demon?"

"No, living things can't go into the Omen Lands, though I do know they used to be allowed in the Underrealm and Halo. Apparently, Angus used to try and bring all sorts of animals home. They didn't do so well with all the energy floating around the realms, so they ended up making laws against bringing mortal animals in. Barsus literally designed the bestial bats so Angus would stop complaining about it."

"Really?"

"Yes, then Coharrus made the bulls for a similar nature, immortal companions for our kinds that served to protect our realms."

"It would be sad to have mortal pets as we are. Their lives are far shorter to us now than they were in our mortal lives. The bats and bulls cannot fall to time like they do."

The trees grew thinner with neatly trimmed branches hanging above a carpet of freshly cut grass. Picnics, laughing college students, and playing children cast their glances at the two. Each pair of eyes completely unaware of the wings they hid.

"We're almost there, the light green house across the street," Airen said.

"Friends of yours?"

"An acquaintance from an evening of answering prayers." She grabbed the puppy from Haven's arms, set it behind the small fence, and tied a small note around her neck. "Stay here. This will be a good home for you."

"Want to say hi?"

"No, we can watch from the park."

The two returned to the shade of the trees, watching the small animal chase butterflies around the yard, leaping and barking without a care in the world.

"What's that?" The door swung open. A small boy ran out and kneeled next to the puppy. "Hi! Where did you come from? How did you get in here?" The dog leapt into his lap, excitedly wagging her tail. "Mom, look! She's so cute. Can we keep her?"

The mother looked around. "How did it get in the yard?"

"I don't know. The note says she needs a good home. Can we keep her? Please."

"Dustin…"

"Pleeeeeeeease."

The woman stared at the small, wriggling dog, eventually letting out a sigh. "Ok."

"Yes!"

"What are you going to name her?"

"Hmm… Airen, after the lady that helped me."

"Sounds good."

Haven nudged Airen's shoulder. "Pretty good name."

The boy lifted the puppy and ran inside. "We need to go shopping!"

"Ok, ok." The mother followed with a smile.

Airen turned toward Haven and grinned. "Seems you have done a good deed today."

"You picked the house."

"What would you have done if I didn't find you two?"

"Probably would have walked around with her for a while, waiting for the right place or person. Could have taken her to Dejen. He knows almost everyone around."

"You still would have saved her. How un-demon of you."

"We love animals…at least, most of us. Were you heading somewhere before we interrupted you?"

"No, just enjoying the sun."

"It's about to set. I know a good place to watch, if you're interested. Not too far a walk."

Airen took her hand. "Sounds good."

The pair meandered through the streets and across a bridge, occasionally catching a glance of shifting shadows, creaking branches, and out-of-place gargoyles.

"The things we never saw..." Airen started, staring at an odd-looking crow. "The life that evaded us, made people tell of ghosts and strange happenings. I wonder how many would be content to know the truth of their shadows."

"That's all the fun, isn't it, making up stories of what you believe is out there? Keeps people creative."

"We do have so many stories."

"Any particular ones you remember from when you were alive?"

"I really liked the old Norse tales, the ideas of other worlds and gods that lived lives full of thrills and hardships of their own."

"Perhaps our Lord has had their share of them."

"I'll ask next time I speak with them. I'm sure they would have limitless stories to tell."

Haven led her through a tall chain-link fence. "This place used to be a park. Those old stones used to be a part of the ranger cabin, the last of the old buildings. They've been building up the area for a few years now."

"People change so rapidly."

"There's still an old watchtower up that hill. Best view in the city."

"I assume that's where we're headed?"

"Yeah... Wait..."

A bright gold and bronze bull stepped out of the shadows. Its head was covered in twisted horns and shining white eyes. Its body was pulsing with unease, scraping against its own movements. Its eyes rolled around in its head. Agonizing screams erupted from its mouth as it charged forward. Haven pulled Airen out of its path, watching the bull crash through the wall. Its screams mixed with the sound of bending metal and crumbling stone.

"What the hell is it doing?"

The bull pushed out of the rubble, turning to face the two. Its metal components began shifting back into place, correcting dents and scrapes, returning its flawless shine. A simple melody flashed into Haven's mind.

Upon the soft grounds of the all-healing Halo where light never breaks,

the gates are guarded by beasts of a bullish nature covered in golden plates.

Everything they see, everything they hear, commanded by those divine,

to guard white wings and saviors' prayers, and keep the gates aligned.

Golden hooves upon the soft ground, standing tall against unending skies.

White eyes that gaze through your terrible fears and uncover all your lies.

Airen dashed out of its path. Scraps leapt onto the beast's head. The bull thundered across the ground, thrashing against walls while the omen dug its claws into its eyes. Glowing white droplets ran down its face. The screams grew louder, filling the air with agonizing unease. The bull turned its horns back and slammed its face into the ground. Scraps faded into a shadow and darted out of sight.

Airen flew into the air, staring down at the golden figure. The bull's body began to glow with an orange molten hue. Its once-vibrant eyes dripped from its metal skull, staining the plates on its face. It turned its head upward and released a bright pulse from its body, knocking Airen out of the sky. The beast charged again, knocking stone and metal through the air. Airen fell back into the rubble, dazed and confused. Her eyes peered into bright white spheres. *Halt, bull... Cease... Why....* She tried to speak, though no sound was heard. Bright red feathers filled her view. The bull screamed with deafening agony. Golden liquid poured from its back, dripping onto the ground in front of her. Its body slowed and weakened. Airen's bright blue staff was embedded in between its plates, pulsing against the bull's energy. Its components loosened and bent, fading with its eyes. For a moment, the world grew dim and colorless.

"Airen?" Haven rushed to the injured angel, kneeling next to her. "You ok?"

"A little dizzy..." Her head rang. Colors began to slowly reappear, bleeding back into the environment. *Bright red, soft...* "Haven..." She reached out, gently stroking stark red feathers. "Did you...fall?"

"No, my wings would be grey, not red."

"I've never seen this."

"No one has." Haven folded them behind her, pain evident in her eyes.

"It hurts? I'm sorry, they are beautiful."

"I'm just an out-of-place demon." She quickly faded them out of sight.

Airen felt something warm drip onto her hand. "Haven, you're bleeding." She stared at a large gash between her ribs. Haven's breathing was labored. Her eyes turned toward the blood-soaked horn of the still bull.

"Fuck." Her vision began to blur. Pain echoed through her head. Her legs grew weak.

Airen sat her down against the wall and kneeled in front of her. "Please, hold still for me." She called for her staff, carefully hovering it near the wound. Haven took a sharp breath, feeling her muscles and bones trying to bend back into place. "I... It isn't working. You should be healed."

"Have you ever healed a demon before?"

"No, but I know it's possible."

"Well, I'm not exactly average."

"I'd like to try something...only for a moment."

"What?"

"I could try again with your wings open. Having them out helps your energy." Airen held her hands, watching with pained eyes. *Please, let me try...*

Haven let out a sigh. "Ok." Her wings unfurled against the wall.

Airen leaned closer, praying for her miracle. She reached out and ran a hand through her feathers. "I'm sorry, darling, I don't know why it isn't working."

"Let me rest for a few minutes."

Airen sat against the wall, snuggling close. Haven's wing slowly moved around her. Red feathers mixed with white. Just as soft and warm as her own. They watched as the bull began to fade, leaving nothing but golden stains against dark grey stones.

Airen looked down at the staff beside her. No trace of bullish blood, not a single dent or scratch breached its glowing blue surface. "Haven...you used my staff."

"Not really, just stabbed it into the thing."

"Did it hurt?"

"No...it didn't sear me."

"That's odd..."

"Yeah...though not the biggest surprise. I am fucked up."

"Just another curiosity to add."

"Could have something to do with us being together. Those things are magic. Maybe there's a protection rule for partners."

"Maybe..."

"Let's get home before any other malfunctioning divinity relics try to kill you." Haven stood up. Her wings faded behind her. Airen helped her through a portal and sat her in bed.

Scraps flew in with medical supplies. Omen shadows darted around the cabin, seemingly curious. Airen grabbed a wet cloth. *I'm not really sure how to do this... Magic has always been easier... Are we supposed to know normal first aid?* She carefully cleaned and wrapped the injury, watching as Haven's body tensed up in pain. "Perhaps a demon curse could work? I'm not the best at this."

"Doubt it."

"We could try."

"I'll go to Cercaius tomorrow. You shouldn't be hanging around with demons with how badly someone's been trying to fell you."

Airen rested her hand on Haven's stomach. "Would any of them try to take advantage of your weakened state?"

"No, they have nothing to gain from harming me."

Scraps sat beside them. His wing was broken, cracking and scraping at every movement. His expression remained still, unconcerned. Not a single sound, no cry of pain. Airen smiled. "At least I can help you." She gently touched the creature's head, watching the wing reform.

Haven slowed her breathing, trying to clear her mind. *Damn bull...* "They aren't supposed to attack angels."

"It wasn't moving correctly. They're usually more graceful. This one was grinding and scraping against itself like it was being forced."

"Only archangels can task them... Why would one want to fell you?"

"I don't know..."

"I never got a name for who tried having the vile demons fell you. They could be the same."

"It is concerning."

Haven laid back and closed her eyes. "This place of death, of fallen things, is yet still safer than even the Halo."

"Do you want to rest? I can stay, if you'd like."

Haven reached out, gently pulling Airen closer. Scraps laid at their feet. Airen stretched out her wing, allowing it to fall over them. Haven took a deep breath, enjoying the quiet sound of their heartbeats. Nothing had ever challenged the Omen Lands for silence. Even the omens made of stone could quiet their movements and leave no trace, nothing to catch the attention of tired ears. The winds themselves refused to move; even as the omens' wings cut through them, silence would remain.

Chapter 15
The Halo's Reflection

The winds of the Halo were always soft and warm, filled with the sound of wings, trickling water, laughter, and magic. Ever moving, ever full of life, though still with its share of challenges and concerns, as those below struggled and fought. Airen walked down the main hall of the research temple, searching for a particular table hidden in a corner by a window that looked out to the soft clouds, a scene that never lost its vibrance of blue and white.

"Gabriel, I am in need of guidance."

He set down his mug and studied the troubled look on her face. "What is it?"

"I was unable to heal a demon last night."

"Strange, you have no healing limitations as a divine."

"She's different. Her wings are red but feathered. Have you heard of this?"

"No...I don't believe I have. Where did you find her?"

"The Omen Lands initially, but that isn't where she was harmed."

"What happened?"

"She helped defend me from a broken bullish beast. I became stuck and was unable to fly away on my own. She got me out but was left injured. My miracle only healed her slightly."

"A bullish beast attacked you! Are you certain of this?"

"Yes. It wasn't moving right. It strained and scraped, screamed agonizing cries. I've never seen anything like it."

"Let us confer with Mary."

Bright bronze, silver, and golden leaves rested against soft clouds and floating water droplets. Few places were as bright—even as the moon claimed the sky, its light would dance across the reflective flowers, shining through the droplets, creating miniature stars in the calm, warm air of the Halo gardens. A woman stood at the center, wearing a shining silver dress. Her long curly brown hair gently swayed behind her. Her eyes showed wisdom and kindness through soft brown colors.

Gabriel approached her. "Mary, we have a distressing matter to discuss."

"Gabriel, Airen, what is concerning you?"

"She was attacked by a bullish beast last night."

Mary's eyes narrowed with concern. "Where?"

"The Mortal Realm," Airen answered. "It appeared suddenly, kept charging for me. I was saved by a demon with peculiar wings. She was injured, and I was unable to heal her."

"Peculiar?" Mary asked.

"Red feathers."

"Red feathers... Is she still alive?"

"Yes, she's resting."

119

"You are certain it was after you?"

"Yes. It didn't acknowledge her until she started defending me. It was scraping and screaming, burning through itself."

"Did you receive injury?"

"Minor concussion, though it faded as I slept."

Gabriel stepped closer to the flowers, rubbing his chin in contemplation. "Bullish beasts are supposed to be incapable of harming angels."

Mary lifted her hand. "Not completely. It is against their creation but not impossible. An archangel can technically command it to slay a lesser...though the act has only ever been performed on those of fallen wings. I cannot imagine why it would target you..." She stared at the floor in contemplation. "I will speak with Coharrus, the creator of the bulls. He may have answers for us. Gabriel, could look into these red feathers? Perhaps the creature was confused; it may not have been able to identify its target." She took Airen's hand. "Please get some rest. Show caution when you leave the Halo."

"Thank you, I will." Airen took a deep breath and walked out.

Mary turned back toward Gabriel. "Has she mentioned this demon to you before?"

"No, though Izeah mentioned that she had befriended one."

"I find it curious..."

"What?"

"She was far more concerned for this demon than for the attempt on her own life."

"Appropriately curious; she is divine."

"Her eyes were drenched in concern when she spoke of her. I wonder how close they truly are."

"Rare, though not completely uncommon for an angel or demon to find companionship in an opposing," Gabriel said. "They are our reflections, after all."

"This is admittedly more complicated than that. An odd demon and a betraying bull... I fear something more complex is following Airen's fate."

"Should we have someone keep an eye on her?"

"Perhaps, though we will want to be cautious. If there is a plot, we cannot risk any uncertain ears getting involved in our plans."

"You don't suggest an angel at fault?"

Mary turned and placed a hand on a shining silver flower. "We were once mortals. We succumbed to the same trials and temptations, and though we have been lifted, still, anyone can fall."

-

Deep red fog swallowed the bar, illuminating its cracked neon light in a thick haze. The door creaked open, allowing the fog to seep in. Cercaius sat on his usual stool, staring down at an old photo. Haven was used to the sight. Every moment he spent alone, his eyes were glued to the image. His hand was quick to hide it away when someone approached, though Haven had gotten enough quick glances from afar to make out the image. Cercaius sat on a park bench next to a man in a long white lab coat. Never once had he been willing to speak of it.

He smiled and shoved the picture into his pocket. "Haven, what sort of beast did you tussle with? Poor thing must have had a rough night."

"A bullish one."

His eyes widened with curiosity. "Was it sent after you?"

"No...I don't think... It seemed broken."

"Did you show it your wings? That might have confused the thing."

"Maybe... Care to spare a curse?"

"Sure." He got out a green vile demon staff and smacked it violently into her side.

"Fuck!" She stumbled back against the bar. Pain shot across her chest.

"Better?" he asked, sipping his drink.

She pulled her hand away from her side. Blood soaked through her bandage. "No."

He put down his glass and stared with concern. "What?" He smacked her again.

"Ah, stop with that!" She stepped back.

"Why the hell aren't you healing?"

"I don't fucking know."

"When was the last time you were healed?"

122

"I don't think I ever have been. Haven't really gotten hurt this bad before."

"Maybe you should talk with Azazel," Cercaius suggested.

"I think I'd rather take my chances with bleeding out."

"You don't get along anymore?"

"He's been too up my ass lately, needs to learn to keep out of my affairs."

"What sort have you been having? Anything to do with that angel you've been sleeping with?"

"He can have all the fun he wants once he gets off his lazy, pathetic ass and gets his own ties to an angel."

"Ok, ok, you're not in the mood. Stay clear of divine relics for a while, would you? I don't want to get stuck with your jobs if you are slain."

"I only take the interesting ones."

"Right, you're too much of a freak to get assigned."

"Jealous?"

"A little," Cercaius responded, "though I think I'd rather keep my ability to get healed. I've got more important dangerous shit to do."

"Good luck with that." Haven stepped through a portal. "And that's exactly why I stay here."

Airen ran up and gently placed her hand on her wound. "Are you...?"

"It didn't work. Fucking hurt, actually. His idea of healing is smacking the person with his staff as hard as he can."

123

"Oh... What about an archdemon?"

"They don't really acknowledge my existence, except one, but I highly doubt she would heal me."

"They have to acknowledge you for tasking."

"I choose what I do."

"You..." Airens wings shifted. Her eyes darted across the landscape. "You aren't assigned?"

"No."

What sort of demon are you...? Airen wrapped her arms around Haven, resting her head on her shoulder. "Are you feeling any better?"

"Hard to recover after being beaten with a fucking demon staff."

"Perhaps you should rest more." Airen took her hand and stepped toward the path. "Or perhaps we should visit the Mortal Realm. Magic doesn't seem to work on you. Perhaps their remedies will."

"Ok."

Airen opened a portal and hid her wings. The familiar warmth of the apothecary shop brought a smile to her face. The air constantly shifted with different scents and shined different colors as the sun moved across the sky, focusing its light on the various items covering the shelves.

Dejen stood behind the counter, staring at a large crystal. "Ahh, one of my favorite couples. Always interesting when you are around. What can I do for you today?"

"Do you have any healing remedies?" Airen asked.

His eyes shifted with concern. "Let me see." He stepped closer and looked under Haven's bandage. "Did you see a doctor?"

"Not a fan," Haven responded.

"Understandable." He stepped toward a nearby shelf and grabbed a small round tin and a bag of herbs. "Here, use this on the injury, and this tea should help. I know you like cinnamon. What happened?"

"An accident with a bull."

"What were you trying to do, curse it? Wow, you sure do lead interesting lives."

"I was trying to get it away from her."

Airen smiled shyly. "It decided it didn't like me."

"Hard to believe; you practically radiate kindness." He gestured toward the back door. "Here, come sit. Relax for a bit."

"I tried patching her up last night."

"Has it been bleeding the entire time?"

"No..." Haven responded. "I...accidentally got hit earlier today. It re-opened."

"You need stitches."

"Can you do that?"

"Well enough, but you really should see a doctor if it gets worse. Stop going places that involve you getting hurt further."

"Yeah, good plan." Haven winced as the needle dug into her skin. Airen scooted closer and grabbed her hand.

"What happened to the bull?" Dejen asked.

"It was sick," Haven responded, "had to be put down."

"Ah, explains why it tried to harm you." He wrapped her injury and wiped off his hands. "Do you live far? You can stay here tonight if you need."

"Not too far. I'll be ok."

"Alright." He looked at Airen. "Make sure she stays resting for a few days. No more wild adventures with dangerous animals, at least for a while."

"Of course."

He turned toward the open door. "The children are home. Looks like we're about to lose our peace and quiet. Get back home and rest. If you need anything else, I'll gladly stop by."

"Thank you, Dejen."

Through a door, down the alleyway, into a portal, back to the calm stillness of home. "Yeah..." Haven started. "Can't exactly have him stop by..."

"If it gets worse, I'll take you back to him." Airen reached for the door. Scraps jumped up, blocking her hand. "Scraps? What is it?" He reached out toward a twisted path. "What, do you want us to follow? We aren't exactly supposed to be going on adventures right now."

"Must be important."

"You should be resting, Haven."

"I'll be fine to do a little more walking. We can go slow."

"Ok."

Scraps darted clumsily through the air, leading them between the hills into a collection of thick, dead trees.

"You know," Haven started, "this place would be great for a horror movie. Even comes with creepy shadowed creatures."

"Do you watch them often?"

"Ginner and I like to go to the theatres every now and again. Nothing really compares to this place though."

Scraps stopped in front of a small, still pond. Bowing in front of it was the bullish beast. Its face was torn. Its left horn stained dark grey. Its eyes still dripped, crying into the water below.

Airen cautiously stepped closer, placing a hand on its neck. "It's strange to see them colorless. How brightly they glow..."

"Everything here fades."

"Even the gods."

"This used to be their land, their home," Haven said. "It once held every color, until it all faded as they did. No longer of true purpose."

"It never lost purpose, just shifted. Now it's a place of peaceful silence, where all can rest and remember. A place of memories. Good and bad."

"And everything in between."

Chapter 16
Lillith

"My Lord... Please forgive me. It was not meant to end in bloodshed."

"I understand. Hold strong your grace, for it is now unstable. It must be corrected. I assure you know what must be done?"

"I will do everything I can."

"Good. Allow this blood to wash away and guide you to repair."

The words sat in the back of his mind, fighting his will to ignore them. *I will not fall. I will repair my grace.* He took a deep breath, fixed his long brown hair, and adjusted his green coat. *Here she is.* "Airen, a word."

"Good morning, Michael."

"I have heard concerning information of late and would appreciate some clarity."

"Of course."

"I had heard of a demon scheme to fell you. There have been words that you have performed intimate actions with one. I understand demons oft leave rumors, though you have been seen frequently interacting with one."

"Yes...I did, though clearly, I have not fallen."

He stepped closer with a look of concern. "Were you forced?"

"No, I was willing. She isn't like the other demons. She has a strong sense of care, especially for the less fortunate."

"You are not being careful enough, Airen. Her plans could have harmed you."

"They weren't her plans. She took the task after it was charged. I fear if the demons originally paid to do it had been allowed, I may have fallen."

He hid the fear building behind his eyes. *What does she know?* A false smile crept over his lips. "Don't let her weaken your grace. Once may be forgiven, but continuation will certainly fade your wings. Step away from her, divine one. Leave her temptations in your memories." He turned around the corner. *There...the conflict is settling...keep her under observation...* He stopped. His eyes widened.

"My apologies, Michael," Izeah said, standing in front of him. "I did not mean to overhear, but...Airen?"

No...no one was supposed to hear... "Yes, brother, it is unsettling. I warned her to avoid this creature."

"But she did not fall? It is odd."

"Her divinity protected her."

"It would seem... Feeling alright, Michael? There is strain in your eyes."

"The rumors of late are troubling. I admit a lack of rest."

129

"Always overworking yourself, brother. Allow me to assist."

"No, I have all the information needed. I just need time to think."

"Do you know who attempted to fell her?"

"No, but I am close. Do not concern yourself, Izeah. You are well-worked as it is."

"Please join me for tea once you have quelled this issue. We may let our woes fade with words of reminisce."

"I look forward to it." *No... No... No...*

-

The light from the window was blocked by a dark red glow. "Bleeding out, darling?"

Haven sat up to face the figure. "Don't suppose you're here to do anything about it, Lillith."

"No, I was simply intrigued to hear. The demon who informed me was unclear of the bull's intentions." She stepped out of the shadows. Blood dripped from her dark red webbed wings. Her eyes glowed an equal color, full of playful confidence. Her long black hair reached down past her waist, and a tight red and purple dress covered her figure.

"It wasn't after me."

"Who, then?"

"Not important."

"You aren't usually so avoidant."

Haven sighed. "Why would a bullish beast attack an angel?"

"An angel, unheard of. Someone up high must have had enough power and reason to command it. Was it agonized?"

"Yes, scraping and screaming."

Lillith sat next to her. "You defended the angel, then? I assume it's the one you've been sleeping with."

"Rumors?"

"I know everything, darling."

"Yet you won't tell me why I have wrong wings."

"They aren't wrong. They are beautiful. You'll figure it out eventually." She leaned closer and gently stroked her arm.

Haven grabbed her hand and pushed it away. "Not in the mood."

"Still won't let me have you? Too loyal your angel, I take it? Fine. Do tell me if you plan on getting into any more fights with divine relics. I'd hate to miss the entertainment." Lillith walked out the door, disappearing into the grey fog.

Fuck...good thing she's gone. Wouldn't want her and Airen in the same room, not yet at least. Speaking of...

"How are you feeling, love?" Airen asked, stepping inside.

"Dejen really knows his stuff. I'm glad mortal remedies can work on us. Have a fun day of prayers or studies?"

"Studies and serious conversations."

131

"About what?"

"Michael told me to stop seeing you. He was concerned about us sleeping together."

"Are you going to take his advice?"

Airen sat next to her and snuggled close. "No, I'm not worried. He's always been more paranoid about demons."

"Did you tell him?"

"No... I'm not actually sure how he found out. He didn't mention it."

"Well, there have been rumors floating around the Underrealm. Lillith came by earlier to appease her curiosity and be a fucking tease with information."

"What did she say?"

"Not much, never does. She likes to toy with people. It's best to be honest with her. She's going to find the truth eventually. Gets her nose into everyone's business for her own entertainment."

"She has a reputation among angels. A cunning, powerful, and manipulative archdemon."

"Spot on."

"So, she knows about us?"

"Yes, she seemed pretty interested. Don't be surprised if you see her lurking in the shadows."

"Intent to harm?"

"Not right now. She'll probably want to see how things go. She rarely shows it, but her rage is unmatched. Push her too far, and she'll slay you in half a second. She loves bloodshed. Her wings and staff are always soaked. It's her show of power."

"Do you think she would talk to me?"

"I'd honestly not risk that."

"Doubting my divinity?"

"No, honey, but I am doubting your reaction to violence. She'll run you through before you have a chance to blink."

"I haven't experienced many other demons. Michael has always preached a disliking for them, though Gabriel is far more open-minded."

"Angels seem to have more conflicting opinions, though you never fight about them. Demons will agree on most things and still beat the shit out of each other for fun."

"Have your fair share of fights?"

"Mostly with Azazel. We get along fairly well for the most part."

"Could I meet him?"

"Preferably not. He would harm you at any given opportunity. One of the more competitive demons."

"Not as conversational as you?"

"Not when it comes to angels. He can be lazy, but if he actually commits, he's quick with a blade and practically radiates confidence, even when getting his ass kicked. Never once seen him...afraid..." Her mind flashed with an image of his bright copper eyes filled with fear. The sounds of rushing water and shadows lingering in the corner of her eyes. *What?*

"Haven, are you alright?"

"Yeah...just sometimes I get strange visions about others. Images of how they died or fell... I'm not sure why."

"How often does this happen?"

"Not too often. It usually happens when I'm talking or thinking about someone. Sometimes it affects my dreams."

"Have any about me?"

"No, I don't often have good dreams."

"Won't invite me into your nightmares?" Airen asked with a playful smile.

"You're too cute to scare me."

"Would you be upset if I said the same?"

"Perhaps. Wanna try it?"

"Later, when you aren't expecting it."

Chapter 17
When the Waters Belonged to a God

Firey brown eyes focused on white wings, cataloging their owner's movements. He raised his vile staff, watching its green colors shift with vibrance. Then, in an instant, it was dark. Fear filled his body. "What?" he fumbled for the wall, trying to stand. His eyes blurred and shook. "My head..."

"What are you doing?"

"Who?" He turned toward a tall red-headed figure.

"Not important to you, vile. What the hell are you doing?"

"Fuck off." He swung his staff.

Haven grabbed ahold of it and tossed it aside. "Answer."

"Who the fuck are you? I have a task to perform."

"What task? Who gave it to you?"

"Why is that your business?"

She got out a strange grey staff and held it to his neck. "Who?"

"What the fuck..." His eyes widened with pain. He choked for air. "Azazel..."

"Harm that angel, and I'll let him shred you." She stepped back.

"What?" Scraps leapt onto the man's face, clawing at his skin. The pair stumbled across the roof, falling over the edge.

Haven wandered over and peered down. "Thanks for the help, Scraps. Keep him busy for a while." She turned back toward the figure he had been watching. *Good, she's still ok. Fuck, that was close... Does Az even do his own work anymore? Where is that asshole? Probably at the docks again.* She opened a portal and stepped out onto the uneven wet boards.

Cold winds and birds flew together above the seas, filling the sky in chaos. A hooded figure stood at the edge of the dock. His mind swirled with adrenalin and fear as he stared at the shifting waves blending into the setting horizon.

"Az."

"Haven? What brings you here tonight?" She got out the grey staff and smacked it against his shoulder. Az fell to the side. "Not looking for conversation then?" He summoned his demon staff and shot a glowing red beam of energy toward her, barely missing. "No wings? Fine, makes it more fun."

She pushed him back against the dock, watching a smile creep onto his face. Fight and fight again. They knew one another's moves, their reactions. Each step was predicted, though still brought the other pain. Omens would often gather, watching the calamity like bored vultures.

"Leave her alone Az," Haven said, stepping back for a moment.

"She's not afraid of us—you made sure of that. Come on, her blood will look so good on the ground."

A strike of thunder, then a muffled rumble as the pair crashed into the water, feeling the cold sting of the ocean. Haven kicked him lower then paused as a sudden chill crept up her spine. *What...?* Her heart began to race. Large black tentacles swarmed her vision for a split second. The sound of struggling; a drowning mortal. The tentacles reached closer. She could almost feel them. *Fuck, this vision again...* She opened her wings, erupting from the water. Her head felt dizzy, her vision blurred and flashed. She tried to focus on her surroundings, watching a shadowed figure emerge from the water.

Azazel slowly walked out onto the dock, soaked and bleeding. "That was more fun when we still had the old gods. Cthulhu was fucking terrifying. You remember them?" he asked, running a hand through his soaked bronze hair.

The vision flashed once more. "Yes..."

Azazel pulled a small squid-like omen off his leg. "These little things aren't nearly as terrifying, not enough tentacles." He threw it back into the water. "You really aren't going to give in on this?"

"No."

"Falling for that angel?"

"You want to try drowning again?"

137

"Nope, already a pro at that." He winked and disappeared into the shadows.

The memory flashed again, she could see him below her, struggling for air. The tentacles wrapped around his neck, dragging him further down. *How do I know...*

-

For most it was a shock, a sense of unsettlement. The instant lack of sound or wind that accompanied each being into the Omen Lands. Even those of wings and magic would still shift with unease in the odd place. The first realm to defy the laws of the world, a taste of something other. Some even feared it, though to Haven it was home.

Airen set down her book and stood. "Haven, are you ok? You're soaked."

"Went for a swim." She tossed the grey staff onto the couch.

"Is that yours?"

"No... I don't think. It comes to me sometimes when I ask."

"Where did you find it?"

"Here, not far from the cabin. Not sure where it came from."

"Can you use its magic?"

"No."

"Strange... It looks more angelic than demonic... The curves and diamond end are similar to archangels'...but the top structure is different."

"I showed it to a couple demons. Azazel thinks it might be a prototype, or it could have been from a slain archangel. Lillith said it suits me perfectly."

"It does. You are strange and more graceful than you should be. I think it's perfect, though if it was from a slain after-being, that might explain why you can't curse with it. Staffs are only supposed to work for their original owners."

"Still comes in handy. Smacked two people with it earlier. Pretty effective."

"Who were you fighting with today?" Airen asked.

"Some lowly vile demon and Azazel."

"Why?"

"He put a hit on you. I wasn't too fond of the idea."

"Oh... Is he the one that's been trying to fell me?"

"No, he only recently became interested after he found out about us. He thinks you'll be easy because you aren't afraid of demons."

"No, but I do respect that most others would be more aggressive toward me."

"Yeah..." Haven sat down.

"You ok?"

"Just tired."

"Come here, then." Airen reached out and pulled Haven closer. "The threats have been dealt with, so we can relax for a while."

Haven took a deep breath and leaned against her. "Ok."

"Tell me more about where and how you found the staff."

"It was sitting against a tree, sparking with weird magic. Stopped sparking when I picked it up."

"How did it feel?"

"Calming, almost."

"Interesting."

"It disappears sometimes. Thought the omens were messing with it, but...I saw it move on its own one day. Flew through a weird magic door that was glowing gold and silver. I've seen it return through the door a few times as well."

"A magic door..."

"Ever hear about those?"

"No."

"Me either. Even Lillith was confused. She hung around for a while, waiting to see it for herself. She even tried going through it, but it closed and disappeared when she got too close."

"I can check the Halo library."

"I doubt anyone up there would know. If Lillith had no clue, no one else is going to."

"Perhaps the Lord would know."

"Perhaps."

Chapter 18
The Beast of a False God

Blood dripped down his leg and shoulder, staining the soft carpet beneath him. Strained wheezes and choking cries echoed through the room. Their eyes were filled with fear. Those still conscious were beginning to fade. Their minds melted into darkness. Some grew panicked as they saw glimpses of dark grey wings and the sharp edge of a staff covered in their own blood.

He couldn't see it. To him it was clean, glowing as it always did, untouched by the world around. He knew what they saw, mortal eyes that did not understand. To them the scene was far more gruesome, for they could still see the ferocity of red, the stark cold demeanor of his feathers, and the ominous aura of green and blue that swirled around his staff. To them it glowed; to him, it was just grey.

Two figures appeared through a door. "What have you done?" the angel asked, looking around at the struggling corpses.

David turned toward her. "They were unworthy of life."

"You cannot decide that! You do not rule them; you cannot kill them. We are here to help better them—even the demons abide by such rules. You are a cruel monster!"

The vile beside her shook his head. "Don't argue. He can't be fixed." He lifted his staff toward David.

He knew there was blood on the floor. He could still feel it. The number of bodies didn't matter, nor the type of blood spilled. His staff glowed and crackled with energy as he dodged the demon's attacks. The angel darted behind him, trying to find an opening. His mind remained calm. No fear or pain. He knew they wouldn't stop. Their eyes were filled with determination and horror. She wasn't the first angel to fear him. He had grown familiar of the panicked stares and lingering glances. *To them, perhaps...I am a beast.*

"Fuck this!" the demon yelled, charging toward David. His eyes burned with magic. Rage dragged him forward.

David closed his eyes and backed away. He could hear the sound of tearing flesh, the stillness of wings. His eyes opened to the still figures of the two. The demon had fallen into the angel. His staff tore into her chest. Hers had rung through his throat. Their eyes faded in unison. Their wings fell limp. He took a breath and watched as their blood mixed into the puddles on the floor.

A beast of a false god.

-

Haven stopped in front of a large, still lake. Small squid-like omens drifted in the waters, circling around a large, crumbling statue. Its body consisted of tangled tentacles twisting around each other before reaching out into the waters. *Wonder how long their arms would be if they weren't tangled at the base.* The sight of it filled Haven's mind with a confusing mix of comfort and unease. *I feel like... You were helping me that day, weren't you? I don't even know what was happening...how it could have happened...but if you were, thank you.*

"What you saw in the memory resembles them?" Airen asked, stepping into the water.

"I think so."

"Are you sure it wasn't an omen? A large one?"

"It didn't feel like one..."

"I do wonder...why have the omens? We were meant to replace the function of the old gods. Do they just want to watch us? Make sure everything goes well?"

"They cared for mortals as much as we do. Even in their eternal sleep, they may still wish to influence what's going on."

"Did they dream?"

"I... don't know. Lillith might."

"I doubt their dreams would have been like ours. They had such strong ties to magic, who knows how they saw our world. They may have even seen the Lord differently. Izeah mentioned that the Lord shows us a form we can understand. They aren't bound to one physical body."

"The gods might have been able to see through that guise."

Airen sat at the shore, allowing her feet to continue disturbing the water. "I wonder why the Lord chose to make us as we are. Magical beings that reside outside of the Mortal Realm. They could have made select humans immortal to preserve the best ideals, or perhaps ruled over people in a more direct manner. People still can't agree on how the world works."

"They probably never will. I imagine even you were stubborn when you were alive."

"A little. I bet you were far more so."

"Wish I knew."

Airen smiled. "Perhaps we'll figure you out some day."

"The mystery is nice. Most angels and demons are too scared to bother me."

"Too strange for them?"

"Just strange enough, I think."

"I wonder what the gods think of you."

"Feel free to ask. Hell, they might actually respond to you."

"I'm not that special."

"A divine that not only gets along with fallens and demons but is willingly sleeping with one? Yeah, nothing special there."

"You are more intriguing. The only one with wings like yours."

Haven let out a sigh. "They won't tell either of us."

144

"It is a fun adventure, though, trying to piece you together. Who knows, perhaps you are a god."

Haven laughed. "I doubt that."

"Airen is not often wrong," David said, walking up.

"I don't know if that would be better or worse," Haven responded.

"We'll never know." He was slow, showing pain. His muscles strained to move.

"What happened to you?"

"Morbius...then Mitis."

"One from each side. Why would Mitis go for you?"

"I've killed too many."

"Those two still alive?"

"No, they were charged to end me at any cost."

"Fuck... How many mortals?"

"Twenty-six. It was a blood market."

"Seriously? I wouldn't have tried to stop you."

"Some think they could have been reasoned with, though I suspected a demon was influencing their targets."

"Probably Liza. She loves torture."

He threw a broken demon staff onto the ground. "She did."

"You fought her as well?"

"She tried to defend the mortals."

Airen stared at the blood-soaked staff, watching its red vibrance fade to grey as it rested against the ground. "How many demons have you slain, David?"

"Seven," he responded.

"How many angels?"

"Four."

She closed her eyes, picturing angel staffs lying on the ground next to lifeless wings. "That's why both sides want you gone. You challenge both of their ideals."

"I don't believe all humans should live, nor do I believe in tormenting those that do."

Airen looked back toward the statue, staring with unease. *The Lord doesn't try to stop him, but others do...*

"What's wrong?" David asked.

"I... I overheard Diona talk about you...the ones you had slain. It was not long after I was cast. I wouldn't put it past her to have sent Mitis after you. She doesn't like that the fallen ones like you can still mess with mortals."

"She has tried to end me several times. Why does this concern you?"

"You are my friend. I don't think you need to be slain. I am still saddened that you have had to slay others, though I believe you mean more to the balance than they give you credit for."

His eyes shifted. For a moment he could swear hers shined blue. "Thank you." He looked back at Haven, seeing strain behind her eyes. "You also appear injured."

"Fought a bull," Haven said.

"Why?"

"It wanted her."

David looked down toward the water. *That isn't correct, unless... I should tell them...though Lillith has my word.*

"What are you thinking?" Haven asked.

"A bull shouldn't attack a divine."

"No."

He looked back at Airen. "Stay quiet for a while. Angels cannot always be trusted as much as you think."

"What do you know?" Haven asked.

"Things are shifting. Betrayal is...easy for some. Look for it." He unfurled his wings and flew off.

Haven sat down. "Might be a good thing that you've been spending so many nights with me."

"I don't feel unsafe in the Halo, even with David's warning... I've always trusted the other angels. We were selected to work together. It's hard to think one is..."

"You did mention how we still feel. We can still change our minds and fall from our places. We can change just as much as the mortals we watch over. Even archangels can fall, honey."

"But which one is falling now? I don't know all of them personally, and Gabriel and Mary don't have any suspects. They are just as confused and concerned."

"Worries me more that the archangels you do trust don't have a clue. Makes me feel better about you living with me."

"You would want that even if my afterlife wasn't in danger."

"Perhaps."

"I don't fear the Halo, but you do feel more like home now."

Haven took her hand. "Good." She gave her a kiss. "You're my home as well."

"Such sweet words, coming from a demon."

"You can have whatever words you like, though I thought you gave up on believing me to be a demon."

"It's still fun to tease you about it."

"Fair enough."

Chapter 19
Ginner

"Thank you for the help," Dejen said, quickly closing the door. "I really need to cat-proof that door. There's too much in here that those rascals can break."

Airen handed him a small grey kitten. "I'm glad to help."

"This should be the last one. Any damage?"

"No, we got them in time."

"Good." He handed her a wide red candle. "Can you get this to Haven? She mentioned she was out the other day."

"Cinnamon?"

"Of course."

"Sure."

"See you around."

The door closed behind her, rattling with a wooden chime. *I'm a lot more colorful with all this cat hair on me.*

"Hello, my darling divine."

"Hello, love."

"You're going to get in trouble if any angels hear you call me that."

"They might just assume we're messing around."

"Maybe."

Airen handed her the candle. "How do you keep these from turning grey? You had a few on the bookshelf back home that never lost color."

Haven pulled a dark red feather from her pocket. "Set them on these. Our wings are immune to the omen grey."

Interesting. I should let Gabriel know so he can update the research books. "Where are you headed?"

"I was supposed to be terrorizing the institution today, but Ginner is nowhere to be found."

"Don't want to terrorize alone?"

"I don't have a proper staff, remember. I can't exactly perform curses."

"Right."

"Scraps does a good job of scaring people, but it's better to have a curse every now and then to keep up the energy."

"Would you like me to help you look for him?"

Haven put an arm around her. "I could never say no to your company. Besides, Ginner's pretty much harmless to angels. He doesn't care about the rivalry. His head is too full of divine science."

"Where should we start?"

"Well, I've been wandering around waiting to feel his signature."

"His signature?"

"Yeah, you know, how you can feel when another after-being is near."

"No."

"You can't?"

"No."

"Oh…"

"How long have you been able to do that?"

"Since I awoke."

"Is that why you seem to find me so easily?"

"Yes. Everyone has a unique signature. I can pinpoint roughly where they are if they are close enough."

"I thought only the archangels and archdemons could do that."

"I'm clearly neither of those."

"Maybe… you are a prototype of sorts? Perhaps that staff is yours. You could be something new."

"Not that new."

"Right…and the Lord doesn't typically hide things from us, at least not things involving our world."

"Hang on… I think I've got him."

"Ginner, where?"

"That old factory."

Tan stones and faded orange paint covered its surface. Rust dripped down from metal window frames and bent doors, bleeding onto the ground. A large plastic sign wobbled in the wind.

"Orange Lake Laboratories. Seems about right for him. He likes to find creepy places in the Mortal Realm to hide in."

"Hide from what?" Airen asked.

"Usually demons that he manages to piss off. His clone experiments can get a bit unpredictable. He's had a few incidents where one attacked someone and they got pissed, so he brings them to some abandoned place to keep working on them."

The door creaked open. Candles lit the hallway, occasionally out-shone by random flickers and flashes from the broken ceiling lights.

"No. No. No." A loud clang followed by rapid footsteps. "Put it down."

"Sounds like he's in there." Haven pushed open a bright orange door.

"Let go." Ginner was in the center of the room holding on to the leash of a small heel hound. The short, stocky grey beast chewed on the chain with one head, while the other turned to growl at the pair.

"What the fuck? How the fuck did you get one of those?" Haven asked.

Ginner blew his scraggly orange hair away from his eyes. "Hey, Haven. I, uh...made it."

"How the fuck...?"

"I found the remnants of one in the study archives. I stole a sample of its blood and made this thingy. What should I name it?" The beast let go of the chain, sending Ginner careening against the floor.

"You ok?" Haven asked.

"Yeah..."

Airen got out her staff, holding it in front of them as the beast stepped closer, baring its teeth. "It doesn't seem happy to see me."

"Those things were used to test warriors' and angels' skills," Haven said, getting in between them.

"Back up," Ginner said, grabbing the chain. "You aren't here to be killed, freak dog." He pulled one face toward his. "You are here for science." He looked back at Haven. "Either of you know how to control this thing?"

"They are supposed to follow the order of the god that made them."

"Well, Anubis made these...but I did make this one specifically... Sit." The beast lowered its hind end to the ground. Ginner grinned and jumped up. "It listens to me! Wow, that makes me feel powerful. The only heel hound alive, and it bends to my will." He made a dramatic pose.

"Aren't they supposed to be a lot bigger?" Haven asked. "Like elephant-sized, not large-dog-sized."

"Yeah...but I don't have as much magic as the gods did, so I could only make a tiny version." He ran a hand down the beast's back. "It's pretty strong, seems to heal very quickly."

"Just don't let Lillith know. She'd take one look at this thing, grin maniacally, then force you to make her one."

"Then he could have a friend..."

Haven sighed. "You aren't supposed to be taking magic like that. We replaced the gods and monsters to give energy back to mortals, not to just turn around and reclaim it all."

"Just a couple of monsters won't hurt... They can belong to either side, so it won't interfere with the balance. I just won't let Lillith find out."

"That's not an option. She knows everything, Ginner."

"What if I just let her babysit him? She can command him for a small bit every now and then. That would appease her bloodlust and give me a break from keeping an eye on him. Win-win."

"Fine, you know what...I'll make a deal with you. Keep it away from Azazel and the archdemons, and I'll help you with Lillith."

"Deal. Why Az, though? Does he want to slay your girlfriend?"

"Yes."

"I could clone her..."

"No."

"But he could..."

"No."

"What if..." His eyes lit up.

"Christ, here he goes."

"What if we could clone the Lord themself? The omens? That would be exciting." He spun around in a chair.

Airen smiled. "Would be pretty crazy if you were able to clone an old god."

"Don't encourage him," Haven said.

He stopped spinning. "I already tried. Their magic, even dormant, does not allow experimentation of any sort."

"Perhaps that's a good thing."

"I can try to clone you, Haven. It might help figure out why you're so weird."

"I don't think there needs to be two of me."

Airen smiled. "Don't want to share me? Not even with yourself?"

"That would be a fun night." Ginner winked.

Haven glared at him. "No. You are only allowed to clone yourself. One of the few tasks I still have charged."

"Pauly said she'd let me clone her..."

"Did you?"

"Not yet..."

Haven sighed. "I'm heading out."

"Here." He tossed her a small pouch. "I got some more for you. You need them more than me, you know, with the whole 'can't curse' thing."

Haven pulled out a shiny, glowing piece. "Thanks. I can give Scraps a break, not that he minds all the extra mischief."

Ginner jumped up. "What if I cloned him!"

"Feed your dog." Haven closed the door behind them.

"Are you concerned?" Airen asked.

"No, he's got a living heel hound. He won't have time to do any illegal cloning."

"It is honestly very impressive and kind of cute..."

"Yeah, he is, for a damned hound."

"Doesn't seem like the omens mind. Scraps didn't bother him."

"True. We should still make sure he doesn't try making any others."

"Do heel hounds get lonely?"

"I'm...not sure. I know Ginner will take good care of it. Might need to do more research on them."

"I can check the Halo library or speak with Coharrus. He knows a great deal about beasts."

"Not sure how I feel about you going near more bulls."

"Right, the library then." Airen pulled her in for a kiss. "I'll see you back home, honey."

-

Airen exposed her wings to the soft, clouded air, smiling at the tall, colorful structure. Deep green jasper stairs led to the main entrance of the Halo library. Solid gold crept through the walls and tree-shaped columns like veins of a great stone beast. Along them were carved pink flowers, mimicking their living counterparts that grew below, displaying the harmony between the natural order and practical design. The architect was often seen swaying around the inner hall, beaming with a smile as she told of the trials it took to build. No matter the eyes of the individual, their wings, or their intent, she would always adore the act of telling her tale, though today her eyes were strained and sad. She sat inside with her hands resting in her short, messy blond hair, staring down at an ancient book.

Airen spoke. "Evening, Galea. Researching as well?"

Galea let out a sigh. "Just...looking into possibilities. Even after thousands of years, there are still oddities that plague me."

"Anything in particular?"

"I lost a friend—two, actually. It was some time ago, but...I still wonder if...what exactly happened." She closed the book and set it down. "It was an accident. Divine relics can be finicky if you try to manipulate them too greatly."

"I'll keep that in mind."

"It's unfortunate. The years I've spent mourning them. I wonder if I will ever feel at peace. I feel like I should have been able to do something. Michael reassured me that all was being done, but...I sometimes wish I could do more."

"Anything I can help with?"

She smiled. "No, dear, thank you for the offer. What are you here for?"

"I was hoping to do some research on the old beasts."

"Curiosity or project?"

"Perhaps both."

Galea stood and turned toward a row of floating shelves. "This way."

"Thank you."

"What guided you toward this particular topic?"

"I met a demon with a particular interest in them and realized I don't know much myself."

"Well, each god made their own beast. Devil daggers were from the red god. Looked like the human's stereotypical goat demon. Then there were the sea serpents, courtesy of Cthulhu. Tiamat made small, fiery dragons, pesky little things. Then there were the eyeless hyena lions, centaurs, heel hounds, screaming vultures, sand sharks, and sun owls. Those were the main ones. The gods liked to make some odd hybrids every now and then to spice things up. I remember when they crossed a screaming vulture with a hyena lion. Humans still have stories of gryphon beasts, even though there was only ever one and it didn't live long. Made quite the impression."

"Unique things tend to do that."

Galea pulled a large red book from a shelf. "Start with this. It has all the base information, written by Gabriel. He may be able to answer any specific questions you have."

"Thank you."

Galea returned to her table. Chatter filled the air as a pair of newer angels walked in, admiring the number of books with wide eyes. For once, Galea didn't approach them. Her typical joyful demeanor washed away as she flipped through the ancient pages, carefully scanning every word.

I've never seen her so down before. She must have truly cared for them... Airen allowed her eyes to wander over the room. Angels fluttered around, grabbing books, reading, and debating with curious eyes and passionate breath. *I don't know everyone... It's still hard to think someone has been betraying. Gabriel had already been considering it when we last spoke. Only archangels can command the bulls...but I know them. They glow with the desire to help people. What would hurting me do to aid that? Is...something wrong with me? I do get along with the fallen and broken ones. Perhaps I'm not meant to know yet.* Her wings drooped down. She turned back toward Galea. *I truly don't think she would try to harm me. Perhaps it would be ok. My instincts have never wronged me before.*

"Do you have another question, Airen?" Galea asked.

"Could I sit with you? I'm feeling a little down as well and thought we both could use some company."

"Of course, Airen. Why would you be down?"

"Someone is trying to fell me. I'm concerned about their persistence."

"I heard about the bull. Gabriel needed help researching. Another divine relic gone wrong." Her eyes shifted with grief.

He trusts her. That's good. I do too. "Is this what caused you to look into the past?"

"Yes. Some similarities between now and then have brought concerns. Michael has been so worried lately, all the stress from Abadon's recent persistence. We thought not to mention it to him. He has been working himself ragged these past few weeks. Izeah's been concerned...

There is strain again, as there was when..." She closed her eyes. "I promise to do what I can to help you, Airen."

"Thank you."

She set down her book. "Now, what beast in particular are you interested in?"

Few things could compare to the laughter of angels, their smiles that could fill a room with comfort. Galea's eyes regained their passion as she told Airen tales of old beasts. Those that once tried to end her, those that fought alongside her, and those that trialed the mortals. Others soon gathered to hear the tales. Old eyes reliving their memories, and new eyes seeing the old ways through that of another. The books were grand and numerous, made with passion and kept perfectly maintained, yet few things compared to the words of another, one who had seen the words play out years prior. To Galea, they were far more than tales. She witnessed the construction of their realms, learned alongside the gods, and gazed into the eyes of many beasts. Each one she would remember. Each would be allowed their own story.

Galea placed her hand on the side of the building. "Many different beasts were sent by the gods to challenge its build. Mostly centaurs and a few eyeless hyena lions. My people worked tirelessly for weeks constructing and defending it. We had to prove its worth, its right to stand among the greatest of minds. All struggles are passable if you truly believe in your actions. That is what we teach to all mortals. That is what gets them through life."

Glad she is feeling better. "I think it's beautiful." Airen gestured toward a pink stone carving. "Did you carve the flowers yourself?"

"Yes, myself and my brother. He was more precise on the shape and size of the petals. I was happy for the uneven edges and curves. Makes them more realistic, I think."

"I agree. I don't believe I've met your brother."

"He is a demon. We were cast opposing, though we still meet to carve and plan structures."

"I'm glad you are able to remain peaceful."

"Our reflections are the hardest to fight."

Chapter 20
Tiamat

Gabriel found himself standing in the gardens, admiring the magically gifted flowers. No soil or pot was needed. Their roots wove down into the clouds, disappearing below. *Even the strongest of winds cannot move them. Not that winds trouble us. The last conflict was some time ago. I hope another is not brewing now.* He sighed. *There is always turmoil, always something to disturb our peace.* He turned toward a white-haired figure. *Ah, just in time.* "Airen, could I trouble you for a moment?"

"Of course."

He smiled and gestured for her to follow. "Mary will meet us in her study."

The room was filled with colorful books, soft warm carpets, and clouded chairs. A space familiar to all newer angels as they frequented her guidance. Mary sat behind a floating marble table, ready with a smile. "Airen, glad to see you."

"You as well."

"Please sit. Izeah overheard a particular bit of information that I believe Michael has already confronted you about. Tell us, what is going on with this demon?"

"I met her when tending to the omens. She has never shown me harm."

"Is this the one with the odd wings?"

"Yes."

"Your relationship to her?"

"It has become intimate."

"When did this begin?"

"A couple months ago. She learned of the charge to fell me and decide to intervene."

"Did she tell you?"

"Yes, she is honest."

"You care for her?"

"Deeply. She cares for the humans almost as strongly as we do. She isn't cruel without purpose or prone to violence. She's far softer than the rest of her kind."

Gabriel pondered. "Perhaps it has something to do with her wings. I have been unable to find any information regarding red feathers."

Mary rested her hand on her chin. "Perhaps it would be worth meeting this demon ourselves. Has she recovered from your incident with the bullish beast?"

"Yes," Airen responded. "It has been slow. The demon curse did not help. She still bears scars."

"Neither angel nor demon could fully heal her... Peculiar."

"Are you concerned?"

She looked back at Airen's pristine white wings. "I was... It's possible we are not meant to understand yet.

Perhaps you are helping this demon better herself." She smiled with relief. "I trust your judgement."

"As do I," Gabriel agreed. "Tell me, though, were her wings feathered before you slept with her, Airen?"

"Yes, she said they had always been that way, though I hadn't seen them myself until after."

"When did she show you?"

"When the bullish beast attacked me."

"Perhaps there is a connection. Someone may view your intimacy with this demon as a threat...though one that would also have control over the bulls is...deeply concerning. I'd hate to accuse any of our brethren, but we will continue to limit knowledge of this. Galea assisted me with research; she has my trust. With her...grief, there is no one I'd trust more to help with this problem."

Mary nodded. "I agree. Unfortunately, until we know further, no other angels are to be told."

"What has Coharrus said?"

"Four bulls were out that day: three accompanied gates, the fourth's location was unknown. It did not return. He showed genuine concern, though I was still careful what information I gave him."

"It's in the Omen Lands now," Airen said.

"Show us." Mary stood from her chair, following Airen through a portal. The bull was unmoved, resting next to its pond. Its torn eyes stared down at its own reflection, no longer bleeding.

Gabriel walked up to it, placing a hand on its stained horn. "Her blood remains..." His eyes shifted with concern.

"What is it?" Airen asked.

"Demon blood should not stain the bull's horns. All blood, no matter its origin, washes away in the omen lands. It is a place of stillness, lifelessness; blood does not belong. It tends to fade away the moment it falls."

"Does this mean...is she not a demon? Does angel blood stain them?"

"No blood should remain."

"She is neither?"

"It is possible, though I have no idea of her creation or purpose..."

Mary's eyes shifted. "Perhaps it is worth discussing with the Lord."

"Have you seen them recently?" Airen asked.

"No, they have been away for a while, I'm sure on important business."

"Do you think they govern over other worlds?"

"It's possible," Mary said, "though they don't speak of their life outside of ours often. They said that we have enough to worry about in our own world for now. They wish us to stabilize our people before worrying about other life."

"Wise ideals."

"Now, let us visit your demon."

-

"Feeling well, Michael? I don't often see you with your wings away."

"Morning, Izeah. I have been reminiscing lately on how simple life was when I was alive. It has felt nice to have them away and soak in the familiarity of feeling mortal."

"Perhaps you should take a mortal vacation. Go down and relax among them for a while."

"Perhaps I will. What are you here for, brother?"

"Abadon has insisted to face you again. He is terrorizing the border with new attacks. Mary might be useful in helping determine what spells he is using this time."

Michael sighed. "I'll fetch her. Can you get some of the newer angels ready? I wish them to learn from this interaction."

"Very well."

Now, where is she? She knows spells better than anyone... He walked over to four glowing orbs in the center of the room and placed a hand near them. *What realm is she in? Wait...the Omen Lands... Her and Gabriel and...Airen... Why? I must know.* He opened a portal, put on a smile, and appeared next to Mary. "My apologies, but we have an urgent matter in the Halo. Abadon has grown restless again." His eyes shifted to the bull. *No... No... Why is it here?* "What is this?"

Mary touched his shoulder. "Do not trouble yourself with it, Michael. You have been overworked as it is. We will take care of it."

His eyes strained as he let out a sigh. "Alright, if you insist. We must hurry."

"Very well." Mary looked back at Airen. "We will continue after."

The three vanished through a portal, leaving Airen alone, staring at the once-lively statue. "No more will you feel the warmth of the sun, beast. No more will you scream." She sat next to it, shifting her eyes toward the pond. "If only you could tell me why you chased me."

"What would be the fun in that?"

Airen turned toward a tall figure. "Lillith?"

"You must be Haven's little angel." Lillith's smile widened. Fresh blood dripped from her wings and twisted red and black staff. Her glowing eyes cut through the dim air.

"Were you watching us?"

"Yes. Not often multiple archangels and a divine visit here together, especially to ponder the death of a bull. Quite the event; even Michael seemed uneasy."

"You know why it's here."

"I do. Our poor darling Haven has been quite agonized recently. Few things compare to the horns of a bull." She circled around Airen, taking in every detail. "You aren't afraid of me?"

"No. I prefer not to jump straight to fear for what I don't yet understand."

Lillith let out a small chuckle, flashing amusement from her eyes. "Words I've heard once before from a peculiar mortal. I wonder if you have the same lack of self-preservation. Were you one to throw yourself into danger for others when you were human?"

"Occasionally."

"Four lives you risked your own to save, though the last one didn't go well. Your niece, was it?"

"Yes."

"I knew you would be cast. Such a soul as yours, they couldn't pass up such an opportunity, one so similar to the man that was lost to the omens. You are so much like him. A pity he was a man, or I would have tried harder to mess with him, corrupt his divine will." She stepped closer. "You, on the other hand, are far more tempting. So close and so calm." She stared into her eyes, watching Airen's reaction. *Her breathing, her focus, the slight change in her eyes refuse to falter into fear. Her heartbeat remains calm.* "No wonder my darling has such an eye for you."

"She spoke of you. Mostly confirmations of Halo rumors."

"Really? What are they saying about me these days?"

"You are manipulative, clever, and love bloodshed. Few angels would dare challenge you."

"Not often I get flattery from an angel." Her eyes broke away, filling with contemplation.

168

"Conflicted?"

"As tempting as you are," she said, brushing her hand against Airen's chin, "I'll leave you to her."

"May I ask why?"

"There are few who are allowed my respect. One demon, one angel, and my reflection."

Airen smiled. "I would hope to gain it myself one day."

Her red eyes filled with action, shifting with her thoughts and ideas. "Why don't we have a chat with our girl, show her how well we get along?"

"Where is she?"

"A fast learner, aren't you? Shifting your questions, assuming I know." She took her arm. "Come along."

"You know why her wings are different."

Lillith's wild grin returned. "I know everything, sweetheart. I saw everything. Every drop of blood."

"You won't tell me either."

The landscape never shifted nor changed with moving waters. Everything was still and calm. Even those of opposing nature refused to fight in the dim grey fog. The only change it saw was from the footsteps of the omens, the cuts from their claws as they clamored among the trees and stones. They alone belonged to the fog.

"It used to be different," Lillith started. "The lands would buckle and shake whenever the gods showed their strength, whenever they commanded the winds to thrash against the ground. More life than even the Mortal Realm, more change and fury than that of a volcano or raging sea.

Here, their powers were unlimited, until they eased completely. It was slow, an ever-creeping vacuum of grey that drained all color and stopped the wind and water. The fires burned out, the plant life died, and those of power turned to stone. An endless sleep for the home of the gods."

"You were there?"

"Yes, I stood with Tiamat, listening to her song."

"Were you still mortal?"

"No, the first of us were made before the fall of the old ones. We were allowed to live aside them for a while, learning how to use our magic and how to govern over the mortals. Once we were strong enough to handle it on our own, they left for their home. We each chose to stay beside them when they faded."

"To keep them company?"

"Yes, though I wasn't the only one. We each stood with our reflection."

"An angel and a demon?"

"Yes."

"Who was yours?"

She smiled and stopped in front of a large tree covered in crumbling ash. "They were unfortunately...removed."

"What happened to them?"

"Unspeakable things." Her grin twisted sadistically. "It was a beautiful day. There was so much blood it rained from the Halo."

"Lillith?" Haven stood nearby, staring with concern. "Airen, are you ok?"

Lillith took a step closer, staring into Haven's eyes. "Don't trust me, darling? I was just telling her how lively this place once was. I quite enjoy her. She reminds me of someone..."

"Alive or dead?"

"The one lost to the omens—" She glared back at Airen. "—though you are far more pleasant to look at."

Airen smiled. "Thank you."

"See," Lillith started, looking back at Haven. "She's polite, not afraid of me at all. You can soften up now. I'll leave you to settle your thoughts." She disappeared into the dark smoke of a portal.

Airen stepped closer and grabbed Haven's hand. "It's ok, she hasn't done anything to harm me. She said she would leave me to you out of respect."

"She respects me?"

"She said she has respect for one angel, one demon, and her reflection."

"We don't have exact reflections... Wonder who the angel is."

"Perhaps David? He is the only angel that brings bloodshed. I'm sure she would be fond of that."

"You're probably right. She loves this realm as much as he does but doesn't have as much free time to linger here. Everything is a task or goal she's reaching toward. Every conversation is a means for information or manipulation, aside from when she talks to the crow omens. She likes to tell them stories and plot her schemes. Her way of telling her adventures to Tiamat. She's proud to be connected to one of the old gods."

"I would honestly do the same."

"To be fair, I would too." Haven stopped in front of a tall statue resting crooked along the path. Large scales covered its body. Four strong legs held it high in the sky. Two large, feathered wings rose from its back. Three menacing dragon heads all twisted in different positions, showing off their once-ferocious demeanor. Its surface crumbled and cracked, missing large chunks, though none laid at its feet. The ground sat clean, not even a single speck of stone from the fallen creature.

"Were you around when they ruled?" Airen asked.

"I... I'm not sure." Haven gazed up at what was left of the statues faces. "They seem familiar, but..."

"When did you wake up in the Omen Lands?"

"Cincarin age."

"After they fell."

"I...feel like I knew them. I can picture how they moved... Tiamat's song. Lillith likes to sing it when hunting angels."

"Oh... Could you sing it to me?"

Firelight on a cold moon knight, fighting the wilderness alone.

Nothing compares, no monsters nor bears, in the hours when you fight for your home.

Shadows of trees on the blood-soaked streets made of stone from the cliffs of death.

Hours of wrongs and winds filled with songs, that's where war belongs.

Conflicts and lies, trust and ties, strengthens the will of man.

Fight for your eyes and the strength to fly so no other will challenge your plans.

Power of many united by few when the fires of war show what's true.

In the eyes of ravens, the heart of wolves, thundering across the field like bulls.

That is where war belongs.

Feathered omens flew overhead, listening to the song. Their heads were shaped like a curved rhombus with three eyes facing forward and two long horns pointing back.

Haven smiled. "Tiamat was seen as an evil force to most. Those that did not believe or properly understand the gods called them a dragon, telling of their fiery wrath."

"Did they really breath fire?"

"Sometimes. They were known to cause battles and bloodshed, testing the strength of warriors. Those who were worthy were allowed to lead their people to victory. Those that weren't became ash."

"They all seemed so lively. Fierce and bold yet understanding and guiding."

"Without them we would have failed."

"Perhaps."

Chapter 21
Red and Green

Red and green, that was all she could see, though not the typical bright colors that decorated homes during holidays. She could see countless shades of green swaying and flowing helplessly in the wind, brightening when the sun peeked through the sky then diming with the cover of shifting grey clouds. There was only one shade of red, dark and thick, bending the blades of grass, pulling them into sticky puddles. She remembered the roar of thunder, the thrashing of waves, though their colors were dull in comparison to the field of corpses before her.

She knew them, their names and faces as clear as day, though not who they were or why they had been slaughtered. Her eyes couldn't move away. Her body felt stiff, burning with pain. Red dripped down her shirt, falling to the soft grass beneath her feet. Her heartbeat stuttered. She struggled to breathe.

"Fuck..." Haven sat up, staring at the cracked wall.

"Are you ok?" Airen asked, scooting closer.

"Just...one of those dreams."

"What was it about?"

"A battlefield full of corpses. It's one I'd had before, several times."

"A memory?"

"It feels like one. I even know their names, but...I can't place the battle. I don't usually get involved in them."

"Can you tell where it is?"

"A field just outside of a city, though not a modern one. Ancient Greek perhaps?"

"So, not a modern battle."

"No, it had swords, shields, spears, and bows. No less bloody than their guns and flames."

Airen gently rubbed her back. "Did it startle you? Your wings are out."

Haven folded one forward, staring at its feathers. "I didn't even notice."

"They don't hurt?"

"Perhaps the dream is distracting me from the pain...actually, I don't think they have been hurting as much lately." She closed her eyes, trying to focus. "Not since you tried healing me."

"Perhaps I was able to heal you, just not in the way I was hoping."

"Perhaps."

"You are tense, take a deep breath." Airen pulled her closer, tightening her grip. She could feel Haven's muscles loosen, her heart slowed and softened. *There you go...* Her eyes shifted to the nearby window. Crow omens gathered on the closest tree, staring in. *Are they curious? Do they watch because of her wings? Perhaps we are entertainment*

176

for them. Thousands of years of whatever they do...
Thousands... "Haven?"

"What?"

"You...said you woke in the Cincarin era?"

"Yeah."

"That was after the ancient Greek times, my love. You would have to be over 2,000 years old to have seen such a battle, yet you woke in the last few hundred... Are you sure it's Greek?"

"I can hear people taking in Greek...screaming..."

"Do you know the language?"

"Yeah, and most others, in fact."

"How long did it take you to learn them?"

"What do you mean? I awoke knowing them."

"Haven... We don't awake with any more information than we had when we were alive. Did you perhaps study language?"

"I don't know..."

Airen leaned against her. "Hmm...so mysterious, my love. Perhaps you could teach me?"

"If you'd like."

"Later. You still need to rest."

Haven laid back, taking a deep breath as Airen laid against her. She knew it was quiet. Only the soft sound of breathing and the occasional rustle of the blanket floated through the air, though her mind heard far more. Loud clanging metal, screams and cries, the words of so many, silenced by sharp blades and arrows, staining her mind red.

Are...all my memories like this? All those visions full of blood and death. Why? She closed her eyes and drifted off. For once, a dream without bleeding fields and bent shields. Her mind wandered a grand building. Soft blankets, furs, and the finest of wines. Brown eyes and shining jewels. The feeling of home. Then, like a wave, everything collapsed. The feeling burst into pain and loss. Eyes plagued by death. There was no blood, just water, a poisoned cup, and a drowning man.

Chapter 22
Once a Mortal

Sometimes the omens sat still in their realm, hiding among the statues and crumbling stones, pretending to be shadows. Their grey and black appearance could easily blend into the fog if they stood in just the right spot. They as well, broken and faded, would return to the still calm of the lands where all is grey.

Perhaps it is all the same. Every grey stone can shift and crumble, but it will make no difference. It will always look the same. Airen tapped her staff against the ground. *Not even my magic can bring color to this place. I wonder if anyone can.*

Her staff dashed from her hand, firmly grasped in the mouth of a shuck. Its ears were torn, its claws were long and ragged, and its eyes were filled with shifting shades of grey.

"What are you... Wait..."

Its legs soared over a thin stream with a calm, unmoving surface sitting on the ground like a jagged mirror. No movement dared unrest it, even as Airen jumped over. *No air, no wind,* she reminded herself.

The shuck darted through a broken stone building with one wall leaning heavily onto the other. Fragments of charred wood covered the floor and jutted out of cracks and crevasses. Small bits of stone fell from above, taunting the two as they scrambled through, trying carefully not to cause a collapse.

Where are you taking me, shuck?

It ran into a field filled with dead flowers of every shape and size. Tall, colorless sunflowers towered over small lilies and dandelions below. Roses crept along the dead trees, dropping petals and crumbling to ash at the slightest touch.

Even death is still stunning in its own way.

The shuck dropped the staff in front of a figure. He was short with dark grey webbed wings and a faded archdemon staff in his left hand. "Ah, this is yours, I assume?" he asked, gesturing toward Airen's staff.

"Yes," she said, picking it up. "Thank you."

"Omens are quite mischievous at times."

"I like entertaining them. They seem to like games as much as we do."

The man rested a hand on the shuck's head. "My name is Judas."

"Airen."

"Glad to meet a divine. Tell me, what brings you out here?"

"I was enjoying a walk. It's quite peaceful here."

"It is. I'm here to visit an old friend." He turned toward a statue no larger than the average man covered in grey robes. It faced the ground with closed eyes and folded hands. "He was kind no matter the situation. Any and all were allowed his help. I was tasked to guide him. Our Lord saw his potential to push humanity out of their aggression. He was one of few mortals to truly get to speak with us."

"You were close?"

"He was my dearest friend. We would bring debate to mortals of ferocious intent, watch the calm soothe those of misfortune, and encourage equality through his words. Of course, mortals no longer remember. They now have their own stories of his power skewed by misunderstandings."

"My parents would praise him, speak of him as a god."

"To some he is. He wished for everyone to understand and be understood. If they could see more than the face in front of them, they would be less likely to show unkindness."

"It sounds like he would have been a wonder to talk to."

"Michael, Mary, even Lucif and Lillith once shared words with him. He was always glad to talk, to seek understanding. He respected the purpose of both of our kinds."

"I have wished that I had been around to meet him myself."

"Technically, you still can." Judas smiled at the statue.

"May I ask why he did not become an angel? Surely, he was divine, far more so than I."

"People not only followed him, but worshipped him, prayed to him. When he died, he took place among the old forgotten gods, watching the people through omen eyes."

"I have not seen any omen from him."

"We cannot see them, only mortals can. They appear as bright orbs guiding people out of danger."

Omens we cannot see?

He turned toward her and smiled. "Do you know why he doesn't fade like the rest? His statue remains untouched by even the omens."

"No."

"What is this land? What is its purpose?"

"A place of quiet...of memory."

"They know him, hundreds of years after he passed. He is still remembered by most mortals, even those who misunderstand him. Over time, the gods have faded from people's minds, slowly shifting further into omens. Someday, they may fade entirely. Even these lands of stillness change slightly as ever. Nothing can stop it."

Bright white feathers approached from the distance. "Airen, Judas."

"Good to see you, Mary," Judas said, nodding.

"You two seem to be getting along."

"We're both the type for conversation."

"Airen does have a gift for getting along with everyone. You aren't the first demon she has befriended."

"Really?"

"She has a gift for understanding."

"A wise divine."

Mary's expression shifted to contemplation. "You have quite the different perspective, Judas. Perhaps you know something of our latest quandary."

"Few things stump you. I'm interested to hear."

"A demon with red-feathered wings whose blood stained the omen lands after a fight with a betraying bullish beast."

He blinked. "Well...that is a surprising number of oddities..." He looked down and rubbed his chin. "I haven't heard of anything related to this before. No word of anyone trying to take control of a beast nor of this particular demon... Are you sure they are one?"

"We aren't certain."

"Well, I cannot speak for those in the Underrealm. It has been some time since I was allowed inside. Perhaps another demon would know more."

"I have considered a meeting with an archdemon, though they haven't shown interest in cooperating with my questions. They seem not to care of this particular individual."

Airen spoke up. "I talked with one the other day."

"Really, who?"

"Lillith. She showed up after you and Gabriel left the bull."

"Did she say anything?"

"She claims to know everything but refuses to tell."

Judas looked at Airen. "Lillith is one of dangerous schemes. If she is behind this, we wouldn't get much information. She's far too clever."

"I don't believe she is behind it. Her words left me to believe she knows what's going on but isn't directly involved. She made it seem more like entertainment to her."

"Do be careful, young one. Lillith is strong enough to fell a divine. Few can resist her power."

"She won't harm me."

"Oh, why do you think that?"

"I respect her."

Judas smiled. "Curious..."

A small flash of light beamed from Mary's golden staff. She let out a sigh. "Seems I'm being summoned again. I was originally hoping to get to meet your peculiar demon, though it seems I've been far too busy of late. I haven't had much time to leave the Halo. Too much is stirring. We'll have to talk again soon. For now, I must return to my duties. A pleasant evening to you both."

"To you too," Judas said with a smile. He turned back toward Airen. "We often meet here to reminisce."

"So, I am not the only one befriending your kind."

"No, though it is rare."

"Were you friends before you fell?"

"Yes, we had quite intense debates back then. Abadon and Michael used to try and keep us apart so they wouldn't have to hear us chatting the night away. It was the only thing those two could ever agree on."

She looked at his wings. "Could I ask how it happened?"

He gestured toward the statue. "I fell to his words. The passion he had in his eyes for the betterment of all people. Before him, I was a trickster at heart. Still am to some degree, though now I tend to trick mortals into improving themselves."

"Fascinating to know that mortals could still have so much influence on us."

"We are here for them, at the end of the day. Our behaviors shape them, and in return theirs shape us."

Familiar... "Your words remind me of someone."

"I assume you speak of David?"

"Yes."

"He and I are similar in our respect for this man. Some even speculate that we changed places in a way. I gave up my aggressions, and he embraced his. Granted, those events were a great many years apart. He is only a few years older than you."

"Do you know why he is like this?"

"Yes, I saw what happened to him. His...life. He once prayed for help, and I was glad to respond."

"You watched over him? Perhaps that is why he is opposing, gifted with blessings from a fallen demon who had no true grace."

185

"Perhaps it is." He closed his eyes. *Glad to know the younger do not all awake with ill intent toward opposing. Perhaps the recent hatred between us is fading. It would be nice. It has been hundreds of years since the last meeting between our kinds. Debated words have since been left to silent schemes. Perhaps she could petition the return of our peaceful interactions.* "You have both David and Lillith's respect. Do oddities often follow you?"

"It would seem so."

"Then you must live an exciting existence."

"Perhaps I do." *He is like Haven but...more content, more certain. He has no desire to return or repair who he is. It seems the fallen are far wiser. I wonder...* "Could I make a suggestion?"

"Of course."

"I believe I know a mortal that you may enjoy. He holds many of the qualities that you admire."

"I am intrigued. Please, lead the way."

The smoke dissipated in front of the apothecary shop. Strong winds battered the flowers placed outside. A few mortals darted in, taking refuge.

"A welcoming place," Judas said, opening the door.

A small group stood around the counter. Dejen's voice was lively as ever, asking questions of the latest tale-bearer. She was an older woman with short, curly hair and faded, blurry eyes. Though her skin shone with a sense of frailty, her words still held their power. "He had blue eyes," she began, "I remember, and for a moment, I swear I saw wings on his back."

"What sort?" a young man asked.

"Feathers grey as can be. He spoke kind words of reassurance while my eyes lost their focus. I'll never forget how bright his were. Bluer than the sky or sea, like the bright feathers of a blue jay shining in the summer sun. The most beautiful eyes I'd ever seen. The last thing I'd seen, so captivating I could never forget."

"Have you seen him since, or, well...heard him?"

"He visits every so often. Doesn't mind my ramblings. Glad to have company these days with how many friends I've lost."

"You are old."

"Ninety-nine. Far longer than you'll get, kid, ha, ha."

A small rumble of chuckling filled the room. Dejen noticed the figures standing at the back. "Ah, Airen, brought a friend? We were just telling stories while the wind passes through."

Judas reached out a hand. "My name is Judas. It's wonderful to meet you."

"Dejen. The feeling is mutual. Care to tell us about yourself? Any friend of Airen is bound to have interesting tales of their own."

"I have many, those of history, magic, and some conspiracies. I would love to tell a few."

Six mortals, a divine, a fallen demon, and a very sneaky kitten enjoyed the evening of tales. The past lives of great

187

mortals, monsters, and those divine. Legends of golden serpents swallowing people whole, hounds hunting angels' white-feathered wings, demons fleeing from winged horses, and songs of the Gods' Realm. To some, only stories, thought Airen and Dejen knew better.

Chapter 23
Metallic Wings

Hot to the touch no matter where they were. Their eyes radiated red, piercing through the dark. Their grey and black metal plates kept them safe in the shadows, though in the land of demons, they needed no place to hide. Most would fly along the border or stand among tall buildings, gazing across the plane.

Haven turned her head away from the bestial bat. "Wish I had one of those with me when that bull attacked. Damn bats are never where they're needed."

Molten metal sparks flew through the air like bright orange stars. Their light slowly faded as they fell to the ground, becoming once again part of the dark.

"Beautiful place," Azazel said. "The lights of the craft, the destruction that goes into making each and every part, and the outcome." He rested his hand against the face of a new beast. The large, metal, bat-like creature still glowed with hot plates cooling in the night air. "Care to try one of these next?"

"Not particularly."

"I think you could take it. You took down that bull no problem."

"None?" She lifted her shirt, showing the large scar on her side.

"Ok...some problem. You know the bats far better. It should be easier for you, honestly."

"I get enough excitement kicking your ass."

"People have been saying you confused the thing, that's why it attacked you, though I feel like there's more to it."

"I don't know who shoved a stick up its ass with my name on it."

"Barsus said you were with that angel the day you were attacked."

"So?"

"Was it really after you? I mean, you don't really go around making enemies of angels, and I was there the day we discovered that the bats and bulls can't see you for whatever fucking reason. So, was it actually after you?"

"No, I just fought the damn thing."

"Why the fuck was it after your angel?"

"I don't know. You hear of any rumors lately?"

"None about felling her, though I did get a fair earful about felling the archangels. Nothing new about that. Your girl is newer and divine, not an easy or well-known target."

"They have to have some reason."

"Whatever it is, it doesn't seem to be floating around down here. Maybe the angels know more; they had to be the one to send the bull."

"Yeah…" Her face darkened with concern.

"What?"

"I…worry sometimes that she's going to get attacked up there, and I won't be able to help her."

"Well…have you ever actually tried going into the Halo? You aren't exactly normal."

"No."

"Worth a try. We know those bulls won't keep you out. Imagine the shit you could pull off if you could get into the Halo. That would be wild… Please punch one of the archangels in the face if you do. I'd love to see that."

"If I do that first thing, they'll be on high alert. I have to be sneaky about it, then I could get away with more."

"Fine, fine, do what you want. Just tell me if you do get in so I can watch you fuck shit up from the border."

"Fine."

"So, how did you get so close to her, anyways? What's the secret?"

"Going to try and butter up your own angel?"

"If you tell me how it's done."

"I didn't exactly plot to get close to her. She just kept showing up, curious enough to talk to me."

"And you persuaded her to trust you."

"She doesn't see sides like most of them do. She doesn't just follow the archangels blindly. She goes out to see for herself."

"Like you, except without the freak wings."

"I don't care to listen. She's curious."

"So, I need to find a newer one with a curious side and relate to them in some way."

"Good luck with that, Mr. Bloodshed Rumors."

"I'll think of something."

They shared a moment of quiet thought, watching the sparks fly around them, listening to the magical hammer tame lively molten metals, forcing them to bend to its wielder's will.

"You show her that weird staff of yours?" Azazel asked.

"It's not mine...I don't think. I just found it. Not like I can use it."

"It's not exactly a demon staff. Looks more like a broken archangel staff. Might be from one of the broken originals."

"Yeah, I guess."

"Can you get any weirder?"

"Don't tempt me."

"You've got to darken up, do more evil. You're missing a perfectly good opportunity with that girl. You should at least fell her, then you won't have to worry about keeping your relationship a secret."

"I haven't exactly been hiding it, and you might recall I did try to fell her...sort of."

"Right, sleeping with her didn't work."

"Just drop it, ok? I have my own path, and I would appreciate you not trying to kill my girlfriend."

He shrugged and turned away. "Wouldn't be the first time."

What? Her eyes flashed again into the cool waters, the image of him drowning below her. *Why were we... What did he do?* A pair of soft, dark brown eyes lingered in the back of her mind, swirling with strong emotions. *Fuck this.* She walked through a portal and sat next to Airen, leaning into her.

"Memories again?" Airen asked, putting an arm around her.

"Yeah. They seem to show up more frequently when I'm with Azazel."

"Do you think he could have something to do with your peculiarity?"

"He knows I'm strange. He was with me the day Coharrus and Barsus held a fighting match between a bat and bull to see how they compared. They do that every hundred years or so. That was when we discovered the beasts don't see me. They had one of each on patrol around the fight, and neither acknowledged me. The bull started chasing Az around. I got a front row seat to two shows."

"They don't see you at all? The one that attacked me...it didn't acknowledge you, did it? It only focused on me and Scraps."

"It only hurt me because I got in its way."

"Another layer of oddities surrounding you. We haven't found answers to any. I'd like to take you to the Lord, but they haven't been around the last couple weeks.

Mary also wants to meet you, but she's been so busy in the Halo. Seems we need to be patient for now."

"If Lillith would stop being a fucking tease, she'd probably be able to answer all of them." Scraps darted in and dropped a note into her hand. Haven let out a sigh. "What now...?" She unraveled the note. "Speaking of Lillith..." She opened a portal and grabbed Airen's hand.

Cold, rusty water dripped down from the ceiling, slowly wearing through the floor. Ginner paced the room, staring as Lillith grabbed ahold of one of the heel hound's heads. "Aren't you a lovely sight, just like your old kin that once roamed the stone cliff lands, challenging mortals and deities alike. A proud use of magic."

"One that won't be repeated," Haven said, stepping closer.

"Hello, my darlings. It's late; did we wake you?"

"Not exactly."

"Oh, were you up to no good? Perhaps a little intimate scandal?"

"Don't be nosey about my affairs. You know enough. We're here about the hound, not our personal matters."

"Everything is personal to someone, dear."

"Is the hound personal to you?"

"He is a magnificent creature capable of tearing apart even the most skilled in magic. Granted, he is far smaller than he should be. It would be a shame to release him in an unsuspecting area... We are the only ones that know of his existence, after all."

"Us and the Lord, though they still have yet to intervene."

"So, we are free to have a little fun."

"What sort of fun?" Haven asked.

"The gates of the Halo have been rather bleak recently."

Ginner hugged his pet. "But they would kill him..."

"True, we would have to get him out before an archangel showed up. Even then, they would search for him." Lillith kneeled and put her head against the beast's forehead. Its body began to glow and shift, slowly altering into the shape of an average dog. "There, I've given him the ability to shift into this more average form. He should be able to blend in for the most part. Archangels and archdemons will still be able to tell he isn't normal."

Ginner jumped up. "Stealth hound! Brilliant, Lillith. Why don't we test him out at the asylum? See how mortals react to him."

Haven closed her eyes for a moment. "Fine." *I can't get five minutes of peace these days...*

"Fuck yes!" Ginner leapt through a portal. The hound chased after, sticking out its tongues and wagging its tails.

Airen followed, listening closely to the echoes of tiled floors and unrest that bounced off the asylum walls. "I don't hear Judy yelling tonight."

Haven stood next to her. "She was discharged a couple days after you helped her. Moved back in with her husband and two kids. No longer chased by bullet-filled nightmares."

"What got her here in the first place?"

"They originally had three children. One was killed in a shooting. She ended up over doing it with anxiety meds."

"I'm glad she's better, though you have one less to torment."

"We had a couple new ones come in. I'm sure they'll get enough nightmares from our new beast."

"Are you going to keep him here?"

"I'll try to convince Ginner to. Not many other after-beings come here, so it would be safe for the hound."

"Cookie."

"What?"

"He named it Cookie."

Haven smiled. "So, these people are going to be having nightmares about Cookie the hound. Great story for them to go home with."

The pair stopped and stared out the window. The east face of the building was faded from years of sunlight. Tall, barbed fences lined the border, showing just as much wear. A place used for modern treatments still showed its aged face and lack of physical change. Those of newer years would find it just as bleak as those from a hundred ago, though now instead of twisting trees they were staring at a false canine. The hound wandered around the perimeter, showing its long sharp teeth. Patients stared out the windows, gossiping in frantic whispers.

"It's just a dog," they could hear the staff say.

Lillith grinned. "It worked."

"What?" Haven asked.

"I enchanted it to follow similar rules of the omens: the patients that are mentally unstable can still see its true form, while the sane ones see a plain dog." Her hands lifted off the ledge as she stepped further down the hall, enticed by the patients' panic.

Airen leaned closer to Haven. "She was able to cast such a strong alteration to it. She is exceptionally powerful. I rarely see the higher ones use their magic, though I had heard of their potential."

"Archangels and archdemons don't use their magic all that often. They only do when its needed, even ones as wild as Lillith."

"Good to know she isn't going around altering things regularly."

"She prefers manipulation. Alterations are more Dominic's thing."

"The grass!" They heard a man yell. "The animals, not just the trees! They're all trying to get us. They want to drive us mad They're everywhere...everywhere!" He sat against the wall, placing his hands against his head.

Airen looked sad. "I know it has a purpose, but...will they truly recover?"

"Not all of them." Haven took her hand. "His name is Murphy Lotsgale. He's been here a while. Did some terrible things to his family. As a punishment, he was cursed to never see the world correctly. He'll keep seeing things no matter what we do."

"I just wish we didn't have to let them suffer like that."

"We aren't meant to kill. At least now his family is safe and happy. I know your kind wish every mortal could be. To be honest, I sometimes do as well, but humans are a rough and ragged species. They have to learn on their own, and sometimes that can be cruel."

The two turned back toward the window. Ginner ran around outside, throwing a stick for the hound. She could see its heads fighting over the large branch, the excitement in Ginner's wings as he leapt out of its path, trying not to get tackled.

Airen smiled. "To him, it's a beautiful evening."

Chapter 24
The Godless War

The field used to be a place of beauty. The unending shades of green dotted in horses, pigs, and cattle. The blades of grass shifted their colors east to the forest and west to the shore as the wind collided with the landscape. Its peaceful, untouched nature once brought calm to busied eyes until red took over green. Again and again, she would dream of it. The faces she could name, the weapons that stole their lives and turned the field, forest, and shore into a place of death.

"Darling..." She could feel a hand rest against her side, the sound of dripping matched with a tall, dark-haired figure.

"Lillith?"

"More nightmares?"

"The same one."

"The war?"

"Yes."

"Hmm."

"Where's Airen?"

"Left about an hour ago to deal with a prayer. Seems someone sunk a large ship not far from the Bryre docks."

Haven sat up and rubbed her eyes. "You've been watching me sleep?"

"I told her that I'd let you know where she was going. I know you've been concerned about her traveling alone lately." She reached toward her waist, gently pressing her fingers into Haven's side. "Still not in the mood?" she asked, watching her move away from her touch. "I just wanted to see how you were doing. You are special to me."

"Why, have a thing for freaks?"

"You know me."

"Well enough to know you're always playing some sort of game. What is it today?"

"I can't just be concerned about you?"

"I doubt you feel concern."

"Don't doubt me, darling."

Haven sighed. "I don't..."

"What is it?"

"I don't make any sense. The things Azazel has been saying, the memories, your weird remarks..." Her eyes softened with sadness. "What am I?"

"I'll tell you...when you no longer need to ask."

"Fine. Why are you here anyways?"

Lillith wrapped an arm around her, pulling her close. "I know who tried to fell your divine."

Haven's expression grew serious. "Who?"

She leaned closer, pressing a soft kiss to her cheek. "Michael."

"Why?"

"Archangels and archdemons cannot be destroyed by simple means. It takes time, effort, and skill. Michael seeks a simpler, more...permanent option. The blood of an angel is highly toxic to demons, especially that of a divine, though little is known about what a fallen divine's blood can do, since there have been no divines to fall. He chose her because she is new and less likely to be noticed missing."

"He plans to fell her for her blood?"

"He had Abadon put a curse on her that her blood will collect in vials when she bleeds. Abadon is cooperating. He knows what this will do to poor Michael. I took the liberty of undoing the curse for you. Wouldn't want his scheme to work this time."

"This time?"

Her grin widened. "Our reflections cause us the most pain." She whispered close to Haven's ear. "You do not appear in her mirror."

What...?

Lillith stepped back. "I'm going to enjoy this. Please let me know when you decide to confront him. It has been far too long since I've seen an archangel fall."

-

The boy bobbed in the waves, struggling to stay up. His tears washed away in the salty waters, blinding his eyes with stinging pain. A large brown dog grabbed ahold of him, dragging him to shore. His mother lifted him up, weeping his name. His hand reached down toward his four-legged friend. "Thank you, Airen."

The dock shook her feet as she watched the scene unfold with a smile.

"It's bound to collapse soon."

Airen turned toward the grey figure. "Thank you for the help, David."

"I am always willing to assist you, especially with so many lives on the line."

"Do you know what caused it?"

He looked up at the sky. "The weather has been temperamental recently. Something feels off."

"Yes, I've noticed. Do you think demons helped it sink?"

"No, I didn't see any. I think this time it was just nature's wrath."

"Good thing it didn't sink too far from the docks, or our job would be far harder."

"I'm surprised we didn't have demon interruption," David said, looking around. "Large catastrophes like this are usually battlegrounds for after-beings."

"Perhaps we just got here soon enough?"

"Perhaps, but I can't shake the odd feeling."

"At least we were able to save everyone. Will you be sticking around?"

"No, there are more cries I must answer." He reached out his hand. "Something for you."

A broken center of an archangel staff? Faded and...grey.

"I found this a few years ago. Lillith asked me not to mention it."

"Haven's staff, the one she found?"

"It has always been hers."

"She..."

He nodded and faded through a portal.

-

Firelight on a cold moon knight, fighting the wilderness alone.

Nothing compares, no monsters nor bears, in the hours when you fight for your home.

Shadows of trees on the blood-soaked streets made of stone from the cliffs of death.

Hours of wrongs and winds filled with songs, that's where war belongs.

Conflicts and lies, trust and ties, strengthens the will of man.

Fight for your eyes and the strength to fly so no other will challenge your plans.

Power of many united by few when the fires of war show what's true.

In the eyes of ravens, the heart of wolves, thundering across the field like bulls.

That is where war belongs.

Haven paced in front of the statue. "What did she mean 'not her reflection'? We don't have exact reflections, it's just a metaphor..." She stared up at Tiamat, remembering their last movements, the song they sang, the figure that stood beside her. *It doesn't make sense...*

Omens stirred with unease. Dark, feathered wings; sharp, cold teeth; moving branches; gargoyles scattered, and even the statues seemed off. The ominous feeling brushed her senses, though this time it was different; uncertain. A deep feeling of dread came over her. Droplets of rain slowly began to circle the statue. One of Tiamat's heads fell to the ground, unfurling into a large, feathered omen. The creature swooped toward Haven, pausing in front of her.

Follow it.

Her wings opened as she ran through a portal, chasing the omen into the city streets of the Mortal Realm. Cold rain poured to the ground. Flickering streetlights and dim windows lit the air. Thunder rumbled in the distance. *These were once the sign of the gods, lightning and unsteady waters. Feelings of dread and doom.*

The omen dashed around a corner, disappearing from sight. Haven took a moment to catch her breath. Her eyes darted toward soft white feathers in the distance. Airen stood near the docks, staring down at the violent waters.

"Airen?"

She turned and smiled. "Haven? Your wings..." Her eyes widened with shock. A bright golden arrow lodged in her chest. Her wings froze. Dark red blood dripped from her shirt.

"Airen!" Haven ran forward, catching her. The arrow faded away. The ocean crashed against the dock, swirling with the winds. Colors faded into a dark grey atmosphere.

The gods are angry, Haven thought, feeling the wind crackle with energy. She knew, as if she'd seen it a hundred times before. *Next will be the...* A bright spark of light hit the ocean, followed by a loud crack and low rumble. Omens shifted through the shadows, filling the air with chaos. She picked Airen up, quickly rushing through a portal. The winds could not follow; instead there was silence as Haven laid her on the bed. Omens swarmed outside of the cabin, creeping in through the cracks in the doors and windows.

Haven grabbed her staff, placing it against Airen's chest. *Fuck, I know I can't, but...* She tried hard to concentrate, though the staff never glowed. Airen's blood continued seeping from her chest. *Shit, I don't have any pieces...* "I don't want to move you too much. Who in the Halo do you trust, someone that would never try to fell you?"

"Gabriel or Mary...but Haven, can you go into the Halo?"

"You do not appear in her mirror."

Haven smiled. "I can." She scribbled a note and handed it to Scraps. "Take it to Lillith."

His wings blended into the atmosphere, nearly invisible in the fog. From afar he appeared as just a man standing in front of a statue. His eyes stared up at its face. He prayed only once in his life, strapped to a table with his heart sliced open. He no longer heard the mad man's judgements, his twisted plans for his latest experiment. The world had gone quiet as he closed his eyes and spoke to those of white wings.

David looked down at the statue's base. "Thank you. Your light was my only solace. You gave me the strength to complete my promise. No matter what deity rules, what gods choose to toy with the world, I will only pray to you."

He saw one that day. He could still feel them. Out of all the angels and demons, he alone was the only one. The small, glowing lights that drifted around the world, helping those in need. He would often watch them with a small smile, knowing he was not alone. He closed his eyes, allowing the silence to return. The sky was void of omens. The ground undisturbed by their feet. Here was a place of true peace.

The sound of drops caught his attention. "Lillith."

"You always know."

"Water does not stir here. The blood you carry is out of place."

"So is yours. Your will is compared to mine when it comes to silencing sinners."

"I do not enjoy the bloodshed."

"No, you are completely indifferent to it. You hardly even notice. Staring at your own blood constantly dripping from your chest made you numb. It became a part of you. Even now you remain covered in it. That is how we are alike."

"Opposing in most regards, but fair. We are equal."

"You are the only one that has never feared me, never once fallen into my games."

"He was like you." The memory was seared into his conscious, ever looming behind his eyes, tainting his vision. A face he could never forget. The face that scared away his grace. The man that feared the shadows. David finally knew why.

"Another angel is due to fall soon."

"He has been corrupting for some time," David said. "His experiments are causing the increase in illfell."

"Really?"

"I can't get close enough."

"I know one who can."

"I assume you have already placed those gears into motion."

"Everything is in order. She only needs one final push." Her eyes drifted back toward the statue in front of them. The only one that had no corrosion, not a single missing piece aside from the hollow eyes none could see. Grey and still, just as the others, though no omens clawed at his surface or rested on his form. "You frequently visit him."

"He answers my prayers."

"So devoted to your false god?"

"Always."

"You would have been like him, if you hadn't been broken."

His eyes turned toward the statue's face. He had never seen him move, never spoke to the man who rested among gods, though his heart was content with the simple glance upon his closed stone eyes. *He needed not to see the world around him, as his eyes became his omens.*

A gargoyle shadow approached them, dropping a note into Lillith's hand. Her lips curled into a slight grin as she read. "This will be interesting." She handed the note to David and vanished out of sight.

I'm going after Michael. I'll try to get him out of the Halo. If I fail, his blood belongs to you, my reflection.

"It begins." He turned down a small path, drawn in a particular direction by a silent call. He knew where they were when they were near, for he alone was allowed to see the fallen man's eyes. He opened the door to an old cabin. A soft, glowing light hovered in the air.

"David?"

"Rest, Airen, it will be alright."

"Haven..."

"She is confronting Michael."

"He's the one that..."

"Yes."

"He's one of the strongest. She might..."

"Her will is far stronger."

Her eyes began to water. Fear crept through them. "David...I'm scared."

"Why?"

"I don't want to lose her."

He looked up at the glowing light. *She still cannot see them.* "Then, for this once, pray to him. Let him guide you as he once did for me." She closed her eyes. He smiled.

"You would have been like him, if you hadn't been broken."

-

Fierce wind cut through the Halo, led by blood red wings. A dim grey staff lunged forward, knocking Michael to the ground. Haven landed in front of him. The room fell to quiet gasps and shocked expressions. Their eyes were immediately drawn to soft red feathers.

"Haven..." Galea spoke, stepping closer.

Haven's eyes remain affixed to Michael. "You tried to fell Airen," she said, standing her ground.

"What?"

"You were the one that paid the vile demons to falter her. You sent the bullish beast after her. You struck her with a divinity arrow."

The room fell to silence. Judgement: he feared nothing more. His wings rested on the ground behind him. Their ends darkened further. Emotions shifted in his head.

Violence raced through his mind. Haven wasn't unfamiliar to it. She had seen it twice before. *An angel falters, breaks under strain. Even the most powerful can succumb to broken choices.*

He stood. "You are out of place, demon…"

"Silence," Gabriel said, stepping forward. "She is no demon." Sorrow and confusion spread across his face. "You know her, Michael. We thought her lost with Joseph."

Haven's eyes blurred. Her head began to ring. *Joseph… I knew…* Bright lights filled her mind. Michael and Joseph stood next to her in a room. Laughter and pride filled the air. It was warm, comfortable, and safe. The lingering feeling of belonging, of home, interrupted by sparks and blood. *"We will help them."* The words were followed by darkness. *Joseph…*

"She fell!" Michael yelled.

"She did not," Gabriel responded.

Izeah stepped closer. "Brother, what is going on?"

Michael's green eyes faltered. "I must…" *Ruined, it is all ruined. They must not listen to her. She is a demon. I am an archangel.* "You will not corrupt me. You will not challenge my divinity." In a flash he summoned his staff, lashing out toward Haven.

She had known violence, pain, and all that the angels avoided, the chaos that he was now losing himself to. Wings tore through the once peaceful warm air. Bright colors flashed off their staffs as they collided. Neither was willing to falter. Rarely had the Halo seen conflict. Angels

210

stood around, watching with shocked uncertainty. Words of betrayal tainted Michael's shadow.

A spark of light blue erupted between them, knocking Michael back once more. Airen stood with her staff glowing. Thick red dripped down her shirt and onto the clouded carpet causing it to glow in a reddish hue. Her legs faltered. Haven rushed to catch her. Michael stood with rage in his eyes, ready to swing. Four archangel staffs pointed toward him. He froze in place.

Mary stepped forward, looking toward his stark grey wings with sorrow. "My friend, you have fallen. No more will you be allowed to harm those of the Halo." She tapped her staff on the ground, opening a portal beneath him. Golden strings of magic wrapped around him, dragging him down. His feathers fluttered in a panic as he disappeared below.

Airen wrapped her arms around Haven, holding tight. "I was right, you are an angel."

"An archangel, actually." Haven looked up at Galea for a brief second, allowing familiar memories to fill her mind. She gazed back into Airen's soft blue eyes. "That's why I couldn't fell you."

"Doubting my divinity?" Airen joked.

"No, yours could never be broken."

Gabriel stepped closer to Haven. "You are the one that Airen has been seeing."

"Yes."

"She is badly wounded."

"She will heal in time." Everyone turned toward the calm, soothing voice. "Allow her rest. She is well cared for." A tall, glowing figure walked into the room wearing a long grey robe. Their eyes shone all colors. Their hair draped down the length of their form; dark as a void at the base, slowly lightening to the brightest of white at the tips. Half-feathered, half-webbed wings rested on their back, clear as smooth glass. "A shame Michael could not undo his wrongs. You were left aside by his mistake, Haven. I tasked him with assisting you, though it seems his fear strangled his grace."

Haven looked down. "I...remember Joseph."

"He is not gone, not entirely. Pieces of him still wander. You found one yourself forty years ago."

Forty...? "Joe Varenfield?" She took the white clover from her pocket, recalling a memory of Joseph sitting in a field of flowers, telling her of their beauty.

"The simplest are still able to shine brighter than those complex. Especially those given purpose."

"He was only a part. You have a gift for finding them." They reached their hand toward a nearby window. "Another has chosen to follow you. One day, he may regain enough pieces to remember."

Scraps flew in, landing in Airen's lap. Haven smiled at the omen. "Got me there, Joseph." She looked back at the Lord. "He felt like an old friend."

"His blood stained your wings."

"I couldn't remember until Gabriel said his name. How many years…"

"Two hundred," Galea responded. "You would still be lost if not for your devotion to Airen." She reached out and took Haven's hand. "I have missed you, my friend."

"I've missed you as well, Galea."

"You were lost? That is why you never returned home? We feared your fate."

"I didn't remember anything. Just a strange demon that awoke from the Omen Lands."

"You fell to the Omen Lands? Michael wasn't sure where you had gone. He said you had most likely been destroyed. We should have looked for you better."

"I'm here now. I know who I am…who I was."

The Lord spoke. "I cannot call you an archangel anymore; neither can I call you a demon."

"Where do I belong, then?"

"Where do you choose to belong?"

She looked back at Airen. "Wherever she is."

"Very well." They turned and walked away.

Galea stepped closer. "Tell us what happened. I fear Michael may have kept information hidden."

"The day I was lost?" Haven asked.

"Yes."

"We discovered that angel blood was harmful to demons. One angel could destroy a demon by sacrificing themselves and binding their blood to the demon. That law was set in place to keep balance. Michael thought he could find a way to use multiple angels, so no sacrifice had to be made. Joseph and I helped with his research. Years of careful planning and study, and we finally chose to test it. They captured Lucif and bound him to the altar just outside of the Halo. He had been doing...concerning things to mortals. We all sacrificed a third of our blood, but the artifacts became unstable, divine blades meant for sacrifice... There was an explosion." She closed her eyes. "I could see my wings...soaked in Joseph's blood... That's all I can recall."

"Do you know what happened to Lucif?"

"I heard later that he was gone. It must have worked, but at the cost of Joseph's afterlife and my removal."

"Everything must stay balanced," Airen said, trying to stand. Her legs wobbled.

Haven tightened her grip. "Easy. We should get you home."

"Where is that, exactly?" Galea asked.

"A cabin in the Omen Lands. It's safe and calm, nothing exciting ever happens there."

"Very well, you may take her. Do come visit. We have centuries to catch up on."

"Of course."

Haven summoned a portal back to the Omen Lands. The silent air and lack of color brought her comfort. "Odd," she started, carrying Airen to the bed, "that this place of passing could be so relaxing. So many things die here, so bleak and colorless."

"Except for you."

"My colors aren't natural. Even my hair used to be different. I was blonde before Joseph fell."

"Do you remember your mortal life?"

Flashes of fire, bright sunlit landscapes, a grand marble temple on a tall hill overlooking the sea, soft brown eyes, and the clanking of weaponry. The sounds were clearer, and the images flowed through her head without strain. "Bits and pieces. I lived back when the old gods still had reign. We would have celebrations in their honor. We feared the lightning, the raging seas, and the twisted trees that moved in the corner of your eye. Life had different meaning back then."

"Where you just as free-spirited?"

"I had a purpose to defend my people and our peace with the gods. I was married to a Greek royal, though I don't remember her name. She was murdered by Azazel. I remember fighting him, then we fell into the ocean. He was dragged under, killed by Cthulhu."

"You never stopped fighting him."

"No, though at least now I remember why. He wasn't made a demon right away. I believe Cthulhu locked him away. The Lord found him later and decided he would be a good demon."

"That's why he didn't know about your wings. He never knew you as an archangel."

"I was still alive when he was locked away."

"How did you die?"

"War." The memory of the battlefield flashed through her mind, clear and bold. "The nightmares...the corpses...they were my people. A rival nation tried to rally against the will of the gods. Me and Joseph were part of an army to stop them. I believe we won. It was named the Godless War. People still tell stories of it. It happened a few days after the Lord arrived. They woke us up and asked us to continue watching over our people. White wings and golden staffs, though our eyes always remain the same."

"One of the original archangels, then?"

"Yes, Lillith's reflection. We stood in front of Tiamat together. She was just as much of a bloodthirsty tease back then."

"Then we do have direct reflections?"

"Only the originals. Joseph and Lucif were reflections, that's why they were destroyed together." She took a deep breath and wrapped her arm around Airen. "So, how did you die?"

Airen leaned into her. "I fell out of a tree."

"Really?"

"I was trying to get my niece down. She twisted her arm climbing up. I remember falling, then I was in the Halo, my brown hair had turned white, bright soft wings on my back, and Izeah's smiling face welcoming me in. He let me go back and calm my niece until help arrived. She was young enough that he was not concerned about her seeing an angel."

"I remember greeting new angels. It wasn't my favorite thing."

"I wouldn't imagine." She giggled. "I can picture you pushing them off the clouds, teaching them to fly."

"Yeah..."

"Did you actually do that?"

"To Mittis...and Guenevere. Michael told me to focus on other tasks after that."

"It's strange to think you were once at his side."

"I don't remember who he was as a mortal, though before the incident, he was driven by justice and peace. We once followed the same path."

"Now you couldn't be more different."

Scraps flew in, landing on the bed next to Haven. Her eyes stared into his for a quiet moment. "Appropriate. Joseph was the one to stand with the red god. Fitting he would inhabit one of their omens."

"I wonder if Lucif is habiting one as well."

Haven smiled. "There is one that hangs out in Lillith's home that...is actually named after him..."

"Sneaky pair, aren't they? Should I expect a crow omen to start following me if you are ever slain?"

"Absolutely."

"Glad to know you'd still hang around, though you are far easier to cuddle as you are now."

Haven kissed her forehead. "Get some rest. All the conflict is over...for now. I'm sure Lillith or Az will stop by some time to bother us with questions. Rumors are probably already floating around."

Chapter 25
David's Heart

Lillith sat on an antique chair, smiling at the sunset. "Always beautiful."

Cercaius approached and kneeled before her. "My task is done. What do you wish of me now?"

"How are my vile doing?"

"Fierce and strong, ready to kill."

"Good. Run them out to a few battle grounds. Let them have fun, appease their desire to slaughter."

He stood and walked out. Lillith reached out a hand to a nearby statue. "Come here, old friend."

The gargoyle leapt onto the arm of the chair. Its legs were scrawny, its horns and tail were long and twisted. Its wings sat motionless on its back, covered in unrepairable cracks.

"Seems we have put everything into motion. Perhaps Haven will have more power in fixing your reflection. You may soon become one again, Lucif." She looked back out the window. "You should have seen it. The spectacle of red wings challenging Michael's already-faltering grace. It was a sight. Shame I couldn't get a closer look. The terror in his eyes would have been priceless."

He nodded and turned to stare at the colorful clouds. Bright orange and pink filled his eyes. Silence took over the room as the pair sat and watched the colors shift ever so slowly. Every second was slightly different than the one before. To them, each moment was just as beautiful.

"It will always change," Lillith said, "as will we."

-

Cercaius walked along the sharp red stones that lined the building. His hand reached into his pocket, pulling out his old photo. "I wish I could have helped you, brother. I wish I could have explained... All those lives you destroyed." He sighed and sat near a garden of thorns. "And what you did to David... What he became. It is your fault he is left in endless pain. Perhaps...it is mine. I could have tried harder to help you, to keep you focused. If Mother could see us now. A dead mad man and a demon." He stared out at the sunset. "I hurt people too, but none nearly as bad as you. Perhaps you were too far gone to become a demon. I'll never know. Lillith will never tell me. You were right, though: I am good at my job. Too good." He hid the photo and closed his eyes. "Goodnight, Harson."

-

Galea sat against the tree. "What are these for?"

Her brother gestured toward the yellow stones. "I had an idea for a garden piece. A large stone mural for the mystic hall. Care to carve more flowers?"

"You have been obsessed with them lately." Galea grabbed a glowing chisel. Her hands moved with exact precision. Thousands of years of practice matched only by the figure that sat next to her. The stone began to transform, creating the soft silhouette of a daffodil. "We found Haven."

Galarro stopped carving. "Really?"

"She was lost to the Omen Lands without her memories. She thought she was an odd demon. Her feathers had turned red."

"My that's...unfortunate, though I'm glad to hear she was reunited with her own kind."

"She is not an angel anymore, not even considered fallen."

"What has she become, then?"

"The Lord didn't specify, though she is allowed to remain."

"That's good. I take it you have spent a great deal of time chatting with her."

"Not yet. She has chosen to stay in the Omen Lands to care for her partner who was injured by Michael just before his fall."

"Ah, so your catching up will have to wait."

"I will wait as needed. I'm just glad she's ok now." She stared down at the stone flower in her hand. "Perhaps you will see her around. Apparently, she can go into all realms."

"Really? I'm surprised I haven't seen her in the Underrealm before."

Galea smiled. "You never look away from your projects."

"Neither do you."

"Excuse me, I look away plenty. With Michael and Izeah busy all the time, Gabriel and Mary running around solving mysteries, Nickolas fallen, Joseph slain, Celenna spending all her time with the mortals, and Haven being weirdly removed, I'm the only one actually around to tell the new casts about our old tales. I'll have you know I've been socializing well."

Galarro sighed. "Our original eighteen have become quite a variety. We are straying further from what we once were."

"But we still hold our purpose strong. No matter how we change, we will always be there for our people."

"That we agree on..." He grinned. "Did you know Ginner made a heel hound?"

"What!? Wait...Airen was asking about the hounds the other week." She sighed and closed her eyes.

Galarro put a hand on her shoulder. "Let them have their fun. The Lord will intervene if needed."

"You're right." She looked over at his work. "I'm still better."

"Don't you start."

"Your usual, or something new?" Dejen asked, holding the teapot.

"My usual will suffice," Judas responded. "How about you, Mary?"

"I have yet to find a tea I dislike," she responded with a smile.

Dejen poured them each a cup. "How have you both been? I understand you recently went through quite the ordeal."

"The loss of a friend," Mary said, "though he may return to us in time."

"I hope things turn out well." He sat down and took a sip. "How are Airen and Haven doing?"

"Well. They have been staying home, resting. Lord knows they need it."

Judas smiled. "They'll need all they can get for the celebration that is going to take place once she is well enough. Triumph over corruption, reuniting old friends, accepting new lovers, strengthening bonds. It will be a truly divine celebration."

"One I wish you could attend, old friend."

"Perhaps someday I will."

"Well," Dejen started, "you'll just have to come celebrate with me instead. My wife loves an excuse to cook up something for the neighborhood. We can have our own get-together."

"Sounds marvelous," Judas said.

Mary grinned. "Perhaps you should invite your friends, Judas. The other fallen. I'm sure they would love to attend."

"Splendid idea. Each realm shall celebrate in unison, as we used to back when the old ones remained."

"Do you remember the food?"

"I could remember nothing else more clearly."

"That is something I miss in these modern days. The simplicity of a well-cooked pig, old wines, the sting of fresh fruit. Perhaps I should invest some time in a new garden."

"I'll gladly help you." Judas closed his eyes and focused on the sounds around. Cats playing under the table, the laughter of his friends, food searing on a hot pan in the next room. *Simple and truly special.* He looked outside at the cold rainy weather. *I am sorry, David, that you no longer have such moments.*

-

They used to be blue. He knew they still were. Just like his mother's and his grandmother's before him. Even as he closed his eyes to remember, they would remain grey. Each memory faded like the new world he saw. *Do I remember what they were, the colors I lost?* He closed his eyes and tried to focus. Memories flashed through his consciousness like an old black-and-white film, rushed and damaged, colorless and cold, though he could still see his family and friends, the people he once knew. As each memory flashed, it was accompanied by pain and images of the reason he lost his colors.

He let out a sigh. *They have embedded themselves together. Memories of good and terrible. I can't separate them. His face is just as clear as hers.*

He closed his eyes once more and allowed the memories to shift wherever his mind wandered. He could see the building, hear it, smell it. The place he wished he could forget was now the clearest in his head. *The day it fell...*he thought, allowing himself to get lost in the memory.

He stood at the end of the hallway, with cold, determined eyes, frightening those that passed by. His right hand clutched his chest, desperately trying to reduce blood loss. Every time he moved too fast or bent down, he had to fight the coughs and wheezes, the pained gasps for air. He stared out the window, watching red and blue lights flash through the gate. Panic. Miscommunication. Mad eyes met with frightened uniforms and cold bullets. The rain began to tap against the glass. He went unnoticed, unbothered. He knew they were falling. He heard every shot, every scream, though he did not flinch, nor turn around.

Everything falls.

The bullets eventually stopped. A single shake of the doorknob, then a muffled voice, before the walls went quiet. Another drop of blood fell from his chest. He waited in the cold darkness with the quiet ticking of a broken clock. Songs and laughter, cries and groans. He knew which ones were ghosts, though he didn't push them away. Reality danced with chilling memories. Hours passed; no one noticed, no one else tried to open the door. Perhaps they were not curious enough. To them, it was done. The place was void of life. Again, he was left alone. He counted the ticking of the clock, clinging to life for the right moment.

Eight hours he stood alone. Eight hours of slow breathing and tired aches. Nothing but the dark and cold tiled floors. He didn't dare move to a bed or chair, or his memories would lash out at him in fear. Ropes, needles, thin cushions, and a blindfold.

"My wandering corpse." The man's twisted smile would never escape his conscious.

He had never known nightmares until the man with a twisted smile ripped him apart. No more did he dream. His unconscious hours were spent in silent absence.

He reached for the door. Blood stains and bullet holes, though he didn't acknowledge them. Four months he spent behind the closed doors and spiked gates. Their structures were now bent and broken, incapable of trapping anything inside.

Is it over? I have to be sure.

The memory shifted and jumped, though he could still feel his chest aching for air. His lungs buckled and trembled. He stood still in the freezing air, watching the rain pull his blood further down his shirt. Muffled voices escaped from a nearby window, anger and frustration in their tone. "Seventeen dead," the police chief repeated over and over, loudening her tone with each word.

He waited for the names: *Jainie Brent, Sal Holmes, Nick Rollhyre.* He knew all of their faces, the sad expressions plastered to each one. The cuts and bruises they held. He refused to forget. *Tim Tomtorsen, Hillary Dunspin, Ashley Fin.* He knew they would fall, those who were too broken down to return, those who had their humanity ripped from them with a scalpel and electric shocks, and those who followed the twisted man, doing his bidding for the sake of broken science.

He stepped closer as the voice settled. *They haven't said my name...or his...*

The chief sat down and stared at her desk. "Five alive, barely. Gina Vest, Shane Colors, Reena Hyme, Rodney Bail, and Harson Grives."

No... The final name echoed in his skull. The man's face flashed into his mind. Maddened eyes and strained words, every movement was commanded with aggression and control. *A man far madder than most of his victims somehow managed to outlive them, to not be killed on sight as the others were. Where...where the hell is he?*

The chief turned toward a large map. "The first four are still in the hospital. Still no sign of the fifth?"

"No," an officer responded. "The ambulance he stole is still missing."

"At least he didn't kidnap the EMTs... Any leads, anything at all?"

"No. We have people monitoring the lab and his home."

"Have people watch the survivors as well. He might try to reclaim them."

"Yes, ma'am."

"He has too much to answer for. Add Gill and Joan to the search team. We need to find him."

They don't know... They don't know...

The rain didn't cease, even as the memory changed. He could see the world fading and shifting until he sat in front of a different building. His eyes shot open as he let out a cough. *Minutes...hours?* He couldn't tell.

The hospital was bathed in the dim, warm lights of windows and short pathway lamps that flickered in the heavy rain. He sat in a bush near the exit, staring down at the ground. His eyes began to blur, his head rang, and his body tried desperately to shake in the cold. Four months indoors, away from the weather, the cold-winded sky. Though his body ached, the storm brought him no real pain. The comforts of a warm, dry space were no longer comforts at all—instead, they only served him a reminder to that still, tiled room.

Crying... He lifted his head, staring at a pair of figures by the door. *Rodney and Reena. Good, they are doing well.*

Her eyes were filled with tears. Rodney did his best to comfort her. "I know, they tried, they really did, she just..." His words failed him. His eyes closed with pain.

Gina... She didn't make it. He could see her face, one of few that still held a smile. The one that never broke, never fell to his madness. *Was she shot? Was she in a lab? Perhaps...she was hiding it, the pain, the madness. She did her best to keep others safe. Now that they are, she can rest.*

Hours... Days... A week? Time had left him. He stood across the road from the fire station, trying to remember where he was and why he had to listen closely.

"Is Reena here?" Rodney asked.

Dina set down her bag. "No, she hasn't been responding, what's going on?"

"Someone broke in, and now her and Shane are missing. That fucker, they shouldn't have left him alive. I'm going to have to kick some ass today. I'm going to get into trouble. Anyone else up for some? I know he took them."

"Where?"

"Get in, fuckers, we're going to fuck someone's day up... We'll have to stop by my place for keys, first."

He...took them? No... David's heartbeat quickened as he jumped into the old truck, racing down the road. Each beat was strained, skipping, and struggling, trying desperately

229

to pump what was left of his blood. *Focus on the road...the trees. Stay awake...Why is the front door open?*

Light emanated from the back hallway. The sound of mad cackling and surgical equipment clanging against a tray. His mind shifted with dark memories. The sounds were all too familiar. His hand tightened against his chest. *No more...*

Harson didn't even hear him. His dusty brown eyes dilated, his hands dropped to his side and his lungs ceased. For a moment he remained standing, staring through void eyes at the woman on the table, until his body finally caught up and collapsed to the floor. Blood seeped from the back of his head, blending into the stained tiles.

David walked up to the figure on the table. "It's alright, Reena. You're going to be ok. Your new friends should be here soon." She leapt up and wrapped her arms around him, quivering and crying. He listened close to her heartbeat. *Quick and frantic but beating normally. Good.* "Just calm down. I'll get you to safety."

He reached into the cabinet and pulled out supplies to bandage her leg. The blood no longer bothered him. His old fears had been pushed back, left in the dark shadows of greater ones. "I'll carry you out. You'll never have to come here again, I promise."

She smiled. "Thank you."

A low rumble rushed across the sky. His arms were going numb. His blood soaked through his shirt. *She has to live...*

A bright orange truck pulled in front of the building. Rodney rushed out. "Reena?"

David set Reena in his arms. "Shane is in the lobby. Get them away quickly." *Get them... to safety...* His eyes blurred, his heart skipped, and his throat strained and tightened, too weak to cough.

"Hey, hey, can you hear me? Can you make it to the truck?"

"No... I have to make sure it ends. Get them out..."

"I can't just leave you here."

"Reena needs medical attention. I have to end this place."

"But..."

"Go."

"Ok." Rodney let out a sigh and ran back to the truck.

Colors faded. His vision began to fail. Darkness surrounded him for a moment, then returned him to the building. Cold droplets fell onto his hand. *It's raining again. Is it fall? I should know...* His legs could barely move, his arms were numb, his eyes could no longer focus. *I have to do this quick, before it gets too wet.* He slowly moved his hand from his chest, grabbing hold of a matchbox. The flame stood out in his vision, dancing around the droplets of rain, refusing to be snuffed out. *No more...* He let go and stepped back. Instead of cackling and crying, there was just the rain, the sound of growing flames, and a soft melody playing in his head.

Away, away, they've all gone away. No need to hide or run or pray.

No ropes and ties will hold you today, for the fires will assure that they never stay.

Time to sleep, time to sleep. No more cries or tears to weep.

Now you can rest your eyes and dream, where once the children wept and screamed.

Away, away, they've all gone away, the nightmares and monsters that forced you to stay.

The hallways are silent, the medicines all gone, no more doctors or nurses to hush you along.

Time to sleep, time to sleep, no more desperate need to leap.

No more pills or wires, aches or pains. No more shocks and burns to your veins.

Away, away, they've all gone away, the nightmares and monsters that forced you to stay.

Now they are safe, now they're ok. No more eyes to fade to grey.

Away, away, they've all gone away. No more madness, no more pain.

It wasn't her lullaby anymore. The months he had spent tied and beaten had twisted it into a maddened song. It used to calm him, the warm embrace of his mother's arms, the soothing of her voice. Everything he saw was accompanied by shadows. Shifting figures that had no care for his fears, hopes, or dreams. They lingered in his memories, making each one more distant and faded every time he tried to reminisce. He could no longer see the once-bright color of his own eyes, for they had been consumed by the monsters in his head. The eyes of his loved ones, those that truly cared and showed him happiness...even his own mother no longer had her own eyes. Instead, they were grey.

His body lay on the ground covered in blood. His eyes were still, only serving as reflections to the fire before him. His heart finally ceased, no more struggling or straining.

All their names sat in front of him, carved onto the wooden structure. Each one who had fallen, lost their minds and lives to the mad man and the bullets that were fired in his name.

"Goodbye, Harson."

The memory faded. David opened his eyes and shifted his wings. *I don't remember how it felt to be mortal. I lived to save the others, I moved to complete my task, I bled till I couldn't feel, and followed the lights only mortals could see.* He placed his hand onto the door of the station and stepped in.

"Rodney!" Dina yelled, chasing him up the stairs.

"I didn't do it! It was Mo or Bobby, not me. You know it was probably Mo, he absolutely would, and he knows more about fire extinguishers. I swear, I didn't know it was fake!"

Three others remained below, laughing at the scene. Bobby and Mo stood by the door with coffee in hand, ready for another day. Reena leaned against the truck, shaking her head. David could feel her happiness, the content in her eyes as she looked out the window. *Thank you, David. I wish you could be here too.*

He smiled. *I will always be there for you, no matter what I become.*

He remembered every second of his casting as clear as day, though he never saw the brilliant gold or soft blue sky, for his eyes could only see grey. At times he could still feel it, the strained pounding of his chest, the blood trailing down his skin. The image plagued him every time he closed his eyes—no matter how many times he would open them and find the wound closed and his heart beating calm, he would always feel the blood.

A small, glowing light caught his attention. It led him through a shifting portal deep in the Omen Lands to an old statue of a serpent beast. Michael kneeled in front of it with tired, confused eyes and dark grey wings. He stared at the creature born from the old gods, one banished long ago by his own hands. It was once his greatest triumph, his trial of worth from the god that trained him, though now he could no longer see its meaning. His grace had left him, his mind was lost to confusion and regret. He didn't care to watch his surroundings. His eyes were filled with tears of uncertainty.

Not the first nor the last to be lost in the lands of omens. David stayed still, watching a figure approach the kneeling man.

"Michael."

"H...Haven, I... What have I done?"

"I forgive you, Michael. You did not mean to harm me...or Joseph. You are my friend. If you need guidance, I will be there for you."

He nodded. His eyes began to water. "Words of an archangel."

"No longer."

A smile fell across David's face. *You do not need to follow a singular path, Michael. Even someone as revered as you. We are not meant to be controlled, but to learn and shape ourselves. Perhaps one day, we will all be grey.*

About the author

Rivara Fall is an author with a passion for peculiar things. Her books fall into several genres including mystery, fantasy, lgbt, sci-fi, and adventure. Born and raised in western Washington, she enjoys rainy weather, playing video games, and spending time with her mischievous pets. Her passions include theatre, science, and art.

If you're interested in seeing her upcoming books, or artistic designs from her stories, you can visit – rivarafall.com

www.ingramcontent.com/pod-product-compliance
Lightning Source LLC
Chambersburg PA
CBHW030111260626
47156CB00008B/2617